CHRISTMAS
KISSES
WITH HER BOSS

CHRISTMAS KISSES WITH HER BOSS

BY

NINA MILNE

MILLS & BOON

First published in Great Britain 2015
By Mills & Boon, an imprint of HarperCollins*Publishers*
1 London Bridge Street, London, SE1 9GF

Large Print edition 2016

© 2015 Nina Milne

ISBN: 978-0-263-26183-7

This one is for my dad,
because I always remember him at Christmas
and always lift a glass to his memory.

CHAPTER ONE

LOITER. SKULK. PANIC. Who knew it was possible to do all three at once? Ruby Hampton shoved her hands into the pockets of the overlong padded coat, worn for the purpose of disguise as well as to keep the bite of the December wind out.

This was nuts. All she had to do was cross the bustling London street and enter the impressive skyscraper that housed Caversham Holiday Adventures HQ. Easy, right? Clearly not, because her feet remained adhered to the pavement.

On the plus side, at least there didn't seem to be any reporters around. Unless they were camouflaged as one of the Christmas vendors touting anything from chestnuts to reindeer-daubed jumpers. Not that she'd studied them too closely as she'd walked through Knightsbridge, head down, in desperate hope that her furry hood and sunglasses would save her from recognition and the mortification of a public lynching.

But so far so good, and maybe the fact there were no paps in hot pursuit meant they had finally got the message and realised that not a single comment would fall from her zipped lips, effectively sewn shut by Hugh's threats.

His American drawl still echoed in her ears.

'One wrong word and my publicity machine will chew you up, spit you out and leave your remains for my lawyers to kick.'

So the paps were better off camping on Hugh's doorstep, where comments flowed in a stream of lies from his glamorous Hollywood lips. No change there. Mind you, she couldn't even blame his legions of fans for their implicit belief in him. After all, she had fallen hook, line and sinker for every honeyed word he'd conned her with. And now...

Now the headlines screamed across her brain.

Ruby Hampton—exposed as two-timing gold-digger!

Hugh Farlane: Hollywood megastar. Heartbroken!

Christmas Engagement Extravaganza off!

Ruby Hampton vilified by Farlane's adoring public!

'Vilified' was an understatement—Hugh's besotted fans were baying for her blood. No one believed in her innocence—instead they believed she had broken Hugh's heart whilst in hot pursuit of filthy lucre. The idea made her toes curl in abhorrence—she'd vowed in childhood never to exist on someone else's handouts and it was a promise she'd faithfully kept. Her parents had produced child after child to reap state benefits to fuel their addictions—had cadged and lied and cheated. No way could she do that.

For a moment shades of the past threatened. Tom… Edie… Philippa… Siblings she'd never see again.

Whoa, Ruby.

The past was over. Done with.

Right now she needed to haul ass and get herself to this job interview—it was time to do what she did best: pick up the pieces and move on. Put Hugh Ratbag Farlane and the past firmly behind her.

Ah…

Therein lay a cracker of a problem—an explanation for her skulk, loiter and panic manoeuvre in blustery December on a London kerbside.

A piece of her past awaited her inside Caversham HQ—a veritable blast from the past was about to interview her.

Ethan Caversham.

The syllables unleashed another onslaught of nerves. The last man she'd ever expected to lay eyes on ever again. The last man she'd *wanted* to lay eyes on ever again.

Get a grip, Ruby—Ethan was so far in her past he was history. She was no longer that wide-eyed teenager with a ginormous crush. Ginormous and short-lived. She still cringed at the memory of that crush exploding into smithereens, bombed by Ethan's words.

'Stop following me around. I don't want your gratitude. I don't want your help. I don't want you. So please just leave me alone.'

Clearly times had changed, because fast-forward ten years and Ethan had contacted her to offer her an interview. His email, via a business media site, had been short and to the point—no hint of whether he remembered her, not much clue as to what the job even entailed. But that didn't matter. Right now she needed a job—*any* job.

She had been a fool to quit her previous job, but she had believed Hugh.

Frustration at her own idiocy clogged her

throat—she'd free fallen for Hugh's persuasive words—had let him mess with her head, believed he needed her by his side. As a result she had given up an incredible job. *Idiot.*

Work was her lifeline—her salvation, her security—and right now no one else would give her so much as an opportunity to ask the time of day. They didn't want to be tainted by all the negative publicity, and she didn't want to sit around and wait until the public furore died down. Not her style.

So... Time to walk the walk, talk the talk and nail this role.

Ethan Caversham meant nothing to her any more—he had walked out on their friendship and as far as Ruby was concerned he was simply a prospective employer with the potential to offer her a job that would enhance her CV.

It would do more than that—crystal-clear determination solidified in her gut. This job would provide her with money and security...the wherewithal to start the adoption process—to have a family. By herself.

Pulling her hands out of her pockets, she urged her feet into walk mode, crossed the street and entered the glass revolving door of the sleek glass-plated building. An elevator ride to the third floor allowed her just enough time to take off her coat and check that the severe professional chignon was still in place, the subtle make-up intact.

The doors slid open, and with a deep in-haul of breath Ruby entered the lobby of Caversham Holiday Adventures.

She braced herself as the receptionist looked up, and on cue there was the expected glare of condemnation. Clearly the svelte blonde woman was yet another of Hugh's legion of fans.

No way would she cower—instead she smiled, and took courage from her carefully chosen outfit: a grey woollen jacket that nipped in at her waist over a tailored black jersey dress. Severe, smooth, *professional*.

'I have an interview with Ethan Caversham.'

The receptionist nodded, tight-lipped. 'I'll let him know you're here.'

'Thank you.'

Adrenalin started to spike and Ruby focused on her surroundings. It was an old childhood trick that had always grounded her in tricky times— helped her concentrate on reality and the importance of the tasks ahead—how to convince social workers that all was well, how to angle a bottle of milk so that the baby didn't cough it up, how to keep her siblings safe…

This backdrop was way different from the squalid environment of her youth—here there was marble flooring, lush green exotic plants, and a lustrous glass reception desk. Imposing photographs graced the walls. Glorious rugged mountains. The turquoise-blue of the sea. A surfer cresting the swell of a wave. The pictures exuded energy and exhilaration.

After a brief telephone conversation the receptionist rose to her considerable height. 'I'll take you to him,' she said.

'Thank you.'

Ruby followed her down a corridor and curiosity, panic and anticipation mingled in her tummy. *Ethan Caversham. Ethan Caversham. Ethan Caversham.* The syllables beat a tattoo in her brain that matched the click-clack of her heels on the parquet floor. Even as she tried to remind herself that he meant zilch to her now.

The receptionist pushed the door open. 'Ethan. Your ten o'clock appointment is here.'

'Thank you, Linda.'

One more censorious look and Linda withdrew, the door snapping shut behind her.

Heart pounding so hard it was a miracle her ribcage remained intact, Ruby stepped forward as a man rose from behind the curved cherry-wood desk.

Oh.

Sure, she'd researched him. Sure, the internet had revealed that present-day Ethan Caversham was hot, rugged and handsome. Come to that, teenage Ethan had been no slouch in the looks department.

But now... Now she was adhered to the plush carpet, mouth agape, as she took in his chiselled features, thick brown hair, cool blue-grey eyes. Six foot plus, with a body that had been honed over the years into muscular perfection. The angry vibe of a decade ago had been muted into an edgy aura of toughness; this wasn't a man you'd mess with.

Nerves that had already been writhing serpent-like in her tummy renewed their snaking.

Come on, Ruby. Don't blow this.

Uprooting her feet, she moved towards the cherrywood desk and held her hand out. 'Ruby Hampton.'

The feel of his fingers round hers brought back a blast of memory and an undefinable, ridiculous sense of safety, and for an insane second she wanted to hold on to his broad, capable hand. For a lingering second his eyes met hers and something glinted in their blue-grey depths.

'Good to see you again,' he said.

'You too.'

His eyebrows rose. 'You don't sound convinced.'

'I...I...'

Oh, for heaven's sake. This was ridiculous. She'd known the past would come up and she'd planned to deal with it with brightness and breeze. Unfortunately the plan hadn't allowed for the poleaxed effect on her of this version of Ethan. What was the matter with her? Instant attraction wasn't something she believed in. Any more than she believed in instant coffee.

'I wasn't sure you knew who I was, given we didn't exactly part on the best of terms.' The words escaped her lips with a lot more tartness than she'd intended—more ice-cold than bright and breezy.

'No.'

There was a pause, but it soon became clear that Ethan wasn't planning to vouchsafe any more. For a moment the urge to berate him—to force an apology for a decade-old insult, a hurt she hadn't deserved—tempted her vocal cords.

Bad idea, Ruby.

The past needed to remain firmly anchored in the past. Plus, no way did she want Ethan to know he could still incite such a seething of emotional turmoil. Truth be told, she wasn't that happy about it herself.

Forcing a cool smile to her lips, she nodded. 'I guess the important thing is that we've both come a long way this past decade.'

He gestured to the chair opposite his desk. 'That we have. Please—have a seat and let's get started.'

Easier said than done.

Annoyance flicked in Ethan at his inexplicable reaction to Ruby Hampton.

Inexplicable? Get real.

Ruby was dynamite. Somewhere in the past decade she had morphed from street urchin to professional beauty—dark hair swept up in a chignon, flawless skin glowing translucent and cheekbones you could climb. The problem was his response was more than physical.

Physical attraction he could deal with—attractive women were ten a penny. But Ruby had awoken something else. Because he'd glimpsed a flash of quickly masked vulnerability in her sapphire eyes. The very same vulnerability that had been there all those years ago. An indefinable yet familiar emotion had banded his chest, and for an instant he could taste those youthful emotions— anger, confusion, panic.

Back then her eyes had held incipient hero-worship too. A look he'd loathed. He had known then, as he knew now, that he was no hero, and the idea of adoration had flayed his soul. Sudden guilt thumped his chest. Pointless guilt. Ten years ago he'd done what had been right for Ruby— ripped her fledgling crush out at the roots before it developed into more. Because then, as now, he had known he couldn't offer more.

Enough, already.

That had been then—this was now. And right now all Ruby's eyes held was a cool wariness as she waited for him to start the interview.

So... 'How did you end up in the catering industry?'

'After you and I...' a small hesitation '...went our separate ways I started a waitressing job and enrolled on an adult education course. I worked every shift I could and studied the rest of the time.' Sheer determination etched her features. 'I wanted out of the hostel and out of the care system. I wanted to make my own way in the world and I wanted to do it as fast as possible.'

'I get that.'

He totally understood the need to spend every second busy, busy, busy, until you fell into bed so exhausted that the past didn't dig its talons into your dreams. He fully grasped the necessity of achieving success for your own salvation.

'Once I got some qualifications the owner of the café I worked in offered me promotion to manager and I took it. From there I moved into hotel work, and...'

As she continued to outline her impressive career trail admiration touched him.

'And your last job was front-of-house manager at Forsythe's?'

Forsythe's being one of London's most prestigious restaurants. Graced by the rich and famous, it adjoined Forsythe's Theatre, run by the Forsythe family for centuries.

'Tell me about your experience there.'

'I worked closely with the manager to give the restaurant a new touch. I introduced a Regency theme—spent hours trawling the internet, art shops and markets, finding some incredible items.'

All wariness clearly forgotten, she leant forward; her hands flying the air as she made a point, her classical features illuminated by enthusiasm as she described finding a genuine two-hundred-year-old sketch of the theatre.

'I researched new menus…liaised with customers—' She broke off and a shadow crossed her face as she sat back in her chair.

'Like Hugh Farlane,' Ethan stated.

'Yes. And many others.' Her tone was noncommittal, her dark blue eyes once again guarded. 'I hope that my experience at Forsythe's ties in with whatever role you have in mind for me?'

'Yes, it does. Let me tell you more about the position.'

And then, if she was interested, he would return to the subject of Hugh Farlane.

'So, how much do you know about Caversham Holiday Adventures?'

'A holiday company with a twist, Caversham offers very high-end packages that incorporate extreme sports and hotels with a difference around the world. Your clients include billionaires, jetsetters and celebrities. Your latest project is a castle in Cornwall.'

'Correct.'

For a second Ethan lingered on his vision for the castle and adrenalin buzzed through him. The brooding Cornish castle had captured his imagination, fired him with a desire to do something different—to mix his business life with his charity work.

'Renovation there is nearly complete, and I'm ready to get the restaurant up and flying. I need a restaurant manager to work with me on the design, the menus and the staff, and to plan a grand New Year's Eve opening. The hotel opens for normal business January fifteenth. I know that's a tight deadline. Especially with Christmas. Can you do it?'

'Yes.' There was not a sliver of doubt in her tone. 'But I'm not sure I understand why you don't already have someone in place.'

'I did. We didn't see eye to eye and he quit.' It had turned out that the guy hadn't bought into Ethan's vision for the castle. 'I've been interviewing for a week or so and no dice. This is an important project and I need the right person. You could be it.'

Her eyes lit up and for the first time since she'd entered the room a small, genuine smile tugged her lips up and sucker-punched him straight in the chest.

'That's great.' Then a small frown creased her brow. 'I can do the job,' she said with utter certainty, 'but as I am sure you are aware I am currently not the public's most favourite person. Social media and the tabloids are awash with vitriol aimed at me—if you hire me there may be a backlash.'

Although her voice was even there was a quickly veiled shadow in her eyes that jolted him. Her words were an understatement—the comments being aimed at Ruby were vicious, awash with menace, and in some cases downright obscene.

Ethan's lips tightened in distaste even as his brain clouded with a black shadow. The knowledge of the tragic consequences that could ensue after such unconscionable bullying twisted his very soul.

Pushing the dark memories away, he focused on Ruby. 'I realise that. It's not a problem. I stand by my employees because I trust them. Which brings me to my next question.'

Her credentials were excellent. Now all he had to do was confirm his gut instinct and make sure he could believe in her.

'Go ahead.' Her body tensed in palpable anticipation.

'Obviously I read the papers, and I've seen the accusations that you are a gold-digger who used your position at Forsythe's to attract Hugh Farlane. At Caversham you would be on the front line, liaising with my clients, so I need to trust that you will be delivering customer service without an eye on their wallets. You haven't denied any of the allegations in the press. Could you clarify the situation for me?'

He leant back and waited for her to do just that.

Instead the smile plummeted from her lips with maximum velocity. Her hands twisted together so tightly that her knuckles clicked in protest, the sound breaking the depth of silence.

Then, 'No comment.'

CHAPTER TWO

RUBY BRACED HERSELF as his brown eyebrows rose. 'You're sure you don't want to expand on that?'

What was she supposed to do? Frustration danced in her tummy even as her brain scrambled for a way to salvage the situation. She knew she was innocent, but logic indicated that she could hardly expect Ethan to give her the benefit of the doubt without some semblance of an explanation.

But there was no way she could risk discussing Hugh Farlane—she *knew* the power he wielded. All it would take was for Ethan to go to the papers with her 'story' and *whoomph*—her life would go further down the toilet.

But, she wanted this job. The thought of a return to her solitary apartment for another ice-cream-eating stint was not an option. However much she liked double-double choc-chip.

Ugh. How had this happened? Ah—she knew the answer. The reason she was in this mess was because she had been a fool—had allowed herself to do the unthinkable and dream. *Again*. Dream that she could have it all—love and a family. *Stupid*. Dreams were fantasies, fiction. In real life she had to concentrate on real goals. Such as this job.

The drumming of Ethan's fingers on the cherrywood desk recalled her to the fact that he was awaiting a response. The slight slash of a frown that creased his brow looked more perplexed then judgemental.

Come on. Answer the man.

'I would like to expand further but I can't risk it. Anything I say could be twisted, so it seems best to me that I say nothing. If you decide to quote me, or post something on social media, it will spark off another barrage of hatred.' And consequences from Hugh that she didn't want to contemplate. 'And I... I don't want that.' She hated that quiver in her voice; she didn't want Ethan to think her scared. 'But I give you my word that if you give me a chance I'll do a fabulous job for you and won't let you down.'

His frown deepened. 'And I give you *my* word that I won't betray your confidence. There is no way that I would aggravate the situation.'

A shadow crossed his eyes and for a second

Ruby saw a depth of pain in his eyes that made her want to stretch her hand across the desk. Then it was gone, and yet the deep sincerity of his words echoed in her brain.

For an insane second she felt the urge to tell him the whole truth. 'I...'

Stop, Ruby.

Had she learnt nothing from the debacle of Hugh Farlane? She'd trusted him and look where it had landed her—up to her neck in metaphorical manure.

Yet it was impossible to believe that Ethan Caversham was cut from Farlane cloth. The man had saved her life ten years ago.

Yes, and then he'd vanished from her life without trace. Cut and run.

But he'd also bothered to call her for an interview.

Head awhirl, she hauled in breath. It wasn't as if she'd be a contender for any Best Judge of Character awards right now. There were times when she still felt enmeshed in the illusions and lies Hugh had woven. So the best rule of all was *Trust no one*.

'Okay.' Ethan raised his hands. 'Think about what I've said. If we're going to work together there has to be an element of trust. On both sides. Now let's consider another of my concerns. I need to know that you would be fully committed to this job.'

That was easy. 'I would be. All yours. One hundred per cent.'

For an instant his gaze locked on hers and the *double entendre* of her words shimmered over his desk. She gulped.

'Yet you left Forsythe's after just two months.'

A flush heated her cheeks. 'That was what I believe is known as "a career mistake".' Of monumental proportions. 'I'd got engaged, and at the time it seemed like the right course of action. The Forsythe sisters were very understanding.'

'I get that. Most women would get carried away by the lifestyle of fiancée to a Hollywood movie star compared to working in an all-hours pressured job. I saw the press coverage of those swish parties—you're clearly a natural partygoer.'

'No!'

The world might believe that of her, but she felt affront scrape her chest at the idea that Ethan should join that bandwagon of opinion.

'I loathed those parties. I'm so used to fronting events or serving tables that being a guest was hard. All that glitter and glam and there was nothing for me to do except—' She broke off.

Except play the part of Hugh Farlane's besotted girlfriend.

How could she have fallen for it? For *him*? At first she hadn't been interested in a man with his playboy heartbreaker reputation. Certainly she had wanted zilch to do with his fame, the limelight, his money. But slowly he'd chipped away at her resistance, and then he'd confessed that he needed her, that she was the one woman who could heal him, and his honeyed voice had called to something in her very soul.

After all, she'd failed to heal her family on so very many levels—with heart-rending consequences.

So when he had gone down on bended knee, when he had poured out his desire to turn his life around, her heart had melted and she'd known she would do whatever it took to help Hugh. And if that meant she'd have to embrace a lifestyle she disliked, play the part of the glamorous girlfriend and smile at the paps, then she would do that. After all, playing a part was second nature to her—and Hugh had needed her.

Yuck! Talk about deluded…

'Except what?' A hint of unexpected compassion softened his eyes as he picked up a pencil and rolled it between his fingers. 'Except be Hugh Farlane's girlfriend? Guess it must have been hard to lose your identity...'

For a second her brain scrambled, mesmerised by the movement and the broad capability of his hand, and shocked by his understanding. For a second the impulse to confide in him returned. To tell him just how hard it had been, and how much worse it had made Hugh's subsequent betrayal.

Swallowing it down, she met his gaze. 'If possible I'd like to keep Hugh out of this. I get that I'm asking a lot, but I promise you can trust me. I will do a brilliant job and I will not leave you in the lurch. Give me a chance to convince you.'

This job was perfect for her—exactly up her street—and her fierce desire to achieve this role had nothing to do with the man offering it. *At all.* All she wanted was to put the last few weeks behind her, to consign the whole Hugh debacle to oblivion and move on.

The pencil thunked down on the table with finality and she felt panic glimmer. She'd blown it.

Silence stretched and yawned as his blue-grey eyes bored into her. Then he blinked, and a slight hint of ruefulness tipped up his lips. 'Okay. I'll give you the job. Trial period until the grand opening. Then we'll take it from there.'

Triumph-tinged relief doused her and tipped her own lips up into a smile. 'You won't regret it. Thank you.'

'Don't thank me yet, Ruby. I'm a hard task master and I'll be with you every step of the way.'

'You will?' Just peachy—the idea sent a flotilla of butterflies aswirl in her tummy.

'Yes. This project is important to me, so you and I will be spending the next few weeks in close conference.'

Close conference. The businesslike words misfired in her brain to take on a stupid intimacy.

'Starting now. I'm headed down to the castle this afternoon. I'll meet you there, or if you prefer I can give you a lift.'

Common sense overrode her instinct to refuse the offer of transport. The only other alternative was a train journey, where the chances of recognition would be high.

'A lift would be great.' The words were not exactly true—the whole idea of time in an enclosed space with Ethan sent a strange trickle of anticipation through her veins. 'Thank you…'

* * *

Ethan gave his companion a quick sideways glance and then returned his gaze to the stretch of road ahead. Dressed now in a pair of dark trousers, a white shirt and a soft brown jacket cinched at the waist with a wide belt, she still looked the epitome of professional. Yet his fingers *still* itched to pull the pins out of her severe bun and then run through the resultant tumble of glossy black hair. Even as her cinnamon scent tantalised…

This awareness sucked.

An awareness he suspected was mutual—he'd caught the way her eyes rested on him, the quickly lowered lashes. So why had he hired her? This level of awareness was an issue—he didn't understand it, and the niggle of suspicion that it was more than just physical was already causing his temples to pound.

Employing someone from his past was nuts—he should have known that. The woman next to him triggered memories of times he would rather forget—of the Ethan Caversham of a decade ago, driven to the streets to try and escape the harsh reality of his life, the bitter knowledge that his mother had wanted shot of him made worse by the knowledge that he could hardly blame her.

Shoving the darkness aside, he unclenched his jaw and reminded himself that Ruby was the right person for the job.

But it was more than that.

The quiver in her voice had flicked him on the raw with the knowledge that she was scared—he'd looked across his desk at Ruby and images had surged of Tanya...of the beautiful, gentle sister he'd been unable to protect.

Of Ruby herself ten years before.

A far scrawnier version of Ruby stood in a less than salubrious park trying to face down three vicious-looking youths. He'd seen the scene but the true interpretation of the tableau had taken a moment to sink in. Then one of the youths had lunged and sudden fear had coated his teeth as adrenalin spiked. Not fear of the gang but fear he wouldn't make it in time.

Once he got there he'd take them on—bad odds but he'd weathered worse. Flipside of growing up on a gang-ridden estate meant he knew how to fight. Worst case scenario they'd take him down but the girl would escape. That was what mat-

tered. He couldn't...wouldn't be party to further tragedy.

The element of surprise helped. The youths too intent on their prey to pay him any attention. The jagged sound of the girl's shirt rip galvanised him and he launched knocking the youth aside.

'Run,' he yelled at the girl.

But she hadn't. For a second she had frozen and then she'd entered the melee.

Ten vicious minutes later it was over—the three youths ran off and he turned to see a tall, dark haired girl, her midnight hair hacked as if she'd done it herself. Her face was grubby and a small trickle of blood daubed her forehead. Silhouetted against the barren scrubland of the park, she returned his gaze; wide sapphire blue eyes fringed by incredibly long lashes mesmerised him. Their ragged breaths mingled and for an insane second he didn't see her there—instead he saw his sister. The girl he hadn't managed to save.

He held his hand out. 'Let's go. Before they come back with reinforcements. Or knives.'

'Go where?' Her voice shaky now as reality sunk in.

'Hostel. You can bunk in with me for the night. You'll be safe with me. I promise.'

She'd stared at his hand, and without hesitation she'd placed her hand in his, that damned hero worship dawning in her brilliant eyes.

Present day, and the end result was he'd offered her a job. Because every instinct told him that Hugh Farlane had done her over somehow. Because he would not leave her prey to the online bullies. Because—somehow, somewhere that protective urge had been rebooted.

The dual carriageway had reduced to a single lane. Dusky scenery flashed past the windows—a mixture of wind turbines and farmland that morphed into a small Cornish hamlet, up a windy hill, and then…

'Here we are,' he said, and heard the burr of pride as he drove down the grand tree-spanned driveway and parked in the car park.

He turned to see Ruby's reaction—hoped she would see in it what he saw.

She shifted and gazed out of the window, her blue eyes fixed to where the castle jutted magnificently on the horizon. 'It's…*awesome*. By which I mean it fills me with awe,' she said.

He knew what she meant. Sometimes it seemed impossible to him that he owned these mighty stone walls, these turrets and towers weighted with the history of centuries, the air peopled by the memory of generations gone past.

Ruby sighed. 'If I close my eyes I can see the Parliamentarians and the Royalists battling it out…the blood that would have seeped into the stone…the cries, the bravery, the pain. I can imagine medieval knights galloping towards the portcullis—' An almost embarrassed smile accompanied her words. 'Sorry. That sounded a bit daft. How on earth did you get permission to convert it into a hotel? Isn't it protected?'

'Permission had already been given, decades ago—I have no idea how—but the company that undertook the project went bust and the castle was left to fall into disrepair. I undertook negotiations with the council and various heritage trusts and bought the place, and now…'

'Now you've transformed it…' Her voice was low and melodious.

Lost in contemplation of her surroundings, she shifted closer to him—and all of a sudden it seemed imperative to get out of the confines of the car, away from the tantalising hint of cinnamon she exuded, away from the warmth in her eyes and voice as she surveyed the castle and then him.

'So, let me show you what I've done and hopefully that will trigger some ideas for you to think about.'

'Perfect.'

The gravel of the vast path crunched under their feet as they walked to the refurbished ancient portcullis. Ethan inhaled the cold, crisp Cornish air, with its sea tang, and saw Ruby do the same, her cheeks already pink from the gust of the winter breeze.

They reached the door and entered the warmth of the reception area. A familiar sense of pride warmed his chest as he glanced round at the mix of modern and ancient. Tapestries adorned the stone walls, plush red armchairs and mahogany tables were strategically placed around the area, with Wi-Fi available throughout.

'This is incredible,' Ruby said.

'Let me show you the rest.'

Ethan led the way along the stone-walled corridors and into the room destined to be the restaurant.

'We believe this was once the banqueting hall,' he said, gesturing round the vast cavernous room also with stone walls and floor.

'Wow...' Ruby stepped forward, her eyes wide

and dreamy. She walked into the middle of the room and stood for a moment with her eyes closed.

Ethan caught his breath—Ruby *got* it. She felt the thrill of this place and that meant she'd do her best.

Opening her eyes, she exhaled. 'I can see how this hall would have been in medieval times. Jugglers, singers, raconteurs—a great table laden with food...'

'Let me show you the other rooms.'

Ruby paused outside a large room adjoining the hall. 'What about this one?'

'You don't need to worry about that one.'

Ethan knew his voice was guarded, but he had no wish to share his full vision for the castle with Ruby. There would be time enough to explain, as and when it was necessary. Right now she was on trial.

'But it looks perfect for a café. Your guests won't always want to dine in splendour—they might just want a sandwich or a bowl of soup. I could—'

'I said you don't need to worry about it.'

Seeing the flash of hurt cross her face, he raised his hand in a placatory gesture and smiled.

'Right now I want you to see the parts of the

castle that I have renovated—not worry about the ones I haven't. Let's keep moving.'

Another length of corridor and they reached a bar. 'I want the castle to be representative of all periods of history. This room shows the Victorian era,' he explained.

'It is absolutely incredible!' Ruby enthused as she stood and gazed around the room before walking to the actual bar, where she ran a hand along the smooth polished English oak.

Ethan gulped, mesmerised as her slender fingers slid its length. He turned the sound into what even *he* could hear was a less than plausible cough. 'Would you like a drink? The bar's not fully stocked yet, but I do have a selection of drinks.'

'That would be really helpful.'

'Helpful…?'

'Yup. Lots of your guests will sit in here before coming into the restaurant. I want their movement to segue. So if I can just soak up the atmosphere in here a bit that would be helpful.'

'Fine by me. What would you like to drink?'

'Tomato juice with tabasco sauce.'

Ethan went behind the bar, ridiculously aware of her gaze on him as he squatted down to grab a bottle, deftly opened the tomato juice, shifted ice and peppered the mix with the fiery sauce.

A blink and she stepped away from the bar. 'You're a natural.' Her voice edged with added husk.

'I make sure I can stand in for any of my staff,' he said, placing her drink on the bar, unable to risk so much as the brush of her hand. He gestured towards an area near the Victorian fireplace, with two overstuffed armchairs.

Ruby sat down and looked round the room, blue eyes widening. 'You have done such a *fabulous* job here—I can't really find words to describe it. I know I've never been to any of the other Caversham sites, but I did do a lot of online research and…' Slim shoulders lifted. 'This seems different. I can't quite put my finger on it but this feels more…*personal*. Does that sound daft?'

No, it didn't. It spoke volumes for her intuitive powers. His vision for the castle *was* personal. And it was going to stay that way. An explanation too likely to open him up to accolades—the idea set his teeth on the brink of discomfort. Even worse, it might pave the way to a discussion as to his motivations and a visit down memory lane.

That was enough to make his soul run cold and he felt his mouth form a grim line.

Ruby twirled a strand of hair that had escaped its confines. 'I'm not trying to pry, but if you do have a different idea for the castle restaurant then I need to know, so I can come up with the right design.'

Time to say something. 'I feel proud of what I've already done here, and I'm sure we can work together to come up with a concept that works for the castle.'

Another glance around and then she smiled at him, a smile that warmed him despite his best attempts to erect a wall of coldness.

'You're right to be proud, Ethan—you have come so far. You said ten years ago you would make it big—but this…it's gigantically humungous.'

There it was again—the tug back to the past. Yes, he'd vowed to succeed—how else could he show his mother, show the whole world, that he was worth something? That he was not his father.

'I'm truly honoured to be part of it. So if there is anything I need to know, please share.'

Share. The word was alien. Ethan Caversham knew the best way to walk was alone. Ten years ago Ruby Hampton had slipped under his guard enough that he'd *shared* his dream of success. And instantly regretted the confidence when it had seemed to make her want more—now here she was again with a request that he share, and once again the promise of warmth in those eyes held allure, a tempt to disclosure.

Not this time—this time he'd break the spell at the outset.

'I do have an attachment to the castle—I think it's because it does feel steeped in history. That's why I've gone into such detail. You may want to take note of the stone floors. Also the reason the room is predominantly ruby-red and dark green is that there were limited colours actually available then. And did you know that it was only in the eighteen-forties that wallpaper was first mass-produced?'

Excellent—he'd turned into a walking encyclopaedia on Victorian restoration.

Ruby nodded. 'You've got it exactly right with the birds and animals motif, and the faux marble paint effects are spot-on too. As for the fireplace…it's magnificent—especially with all the dried flowers.'

Clearly Ruby had decided to humour the boss and join in with the fact-bombardment.

'I love the brass light fittings as well. And all the ornaments. The Victorians *loved* ornaments.' She rose from the sofa and crouched down in front of one of a pair of porcelain dogs on either side of the fireplace. 'These are a real find. A proper matching pair.'

'They are,' Ethan agreed. 'How come you're so knowledgeable?'

'We looked into the idea of going Victorian in Forsythe's.'

That seemed to cover Victoriana, and suddenly the atmosphere thickened.

Rising to her feet, Ruby reached out for her glass, drained it and glanced at her watch. 'Would it be okay if I clocked off for today? I need to sort out somewhere to stay—I've got a list of places to ring.'

For a fraction of a second a shadow crossed her sapphire eyes. Then the hint of vulnerability was blinked away as she straightened her shoulders and smiled at him.

'I'll call them, find somewhere, and then grab a taxi.'

Realisation crashed down. She was scared—

and who could blame her? Right now the idea of an encounter with the public was enough to daunt the staunchest of celebrities.

That instinctive need to protect her surged up and triggered his vocal cords. 'Or you could stay here.'

CHAPTER THREE

'HERE?' RELIEF TOUCHED RUBY, but before she could succumb she forced her brain to think mode. 'Why?'

Ethan shrugged. 'It makes sense. It's a hotel. There's plenty of room. You'll have to make your own bed, and there's no housekeeping service, but you can have a suite and work more effectively here. I'll be staying here too, so you won't be on your own.'

Thoughts scrambled round her brain. Truth be told, she would feel safer here. *Because of Ethan.* The thought sneaked in and she dismissed it instantly. This was zip to do with Ethan—sheer logic dictated she should stay in the castle. Nothing to do with his aura, or the slow burn of the atmosphere.

'Thank you, Ethan. If you're sure.'

'I'm sure. Let's find you a bedroom.'

'Um… Okay.' *Freaking great*—here came a tidal wave blush adolescent-style at the word.

How ridiculous. As preposterous as the thud of her heart as she followed him up the sweep of the magnificent staircase to the second floor, where he pushed open a door marked 'Elizabethan Suite' and stood back to let her enter.

'Whoa!' The room was stunning, a panorama of resplendence, and yet despite its space, despite the splendour of the brocade curtains and the gorgeous wall-hangings that depicted scenes of verdure, her eyes were drawn with mesmerising force to the bed. Four-poster, awash with luxurious draperies—but right now all she could concentrate on was the fact that it was a bed.

For a crazy moment her mind raced to create an age-old formula; her body brazenly—*foolishly*—wanted to act on an instinct older than time. And for one ephemeral heartbeat his pupils darkened to slate-grey and she believed that insanity must be contagious…believed that he would close the gap between them.

Then Ethan stepped back and the instant dissolved, leaving a sizzle in the air. A swivel of the heel and he'd turned to the door.

'I'll meet you in the morning to finish showing you around. If you're hungry there's some basic food stuff in the kitchen.'

'Okay.' Though her appetite had deserted her—pushed aside by the spin of emotions Ethan had unleashed.

'If you need anything you've got my mobile number. My suite is on the next floor. No one knows you're here, so you can sleep easy.'

For the first time in the two horrendous weeks since she'd walked in on Hugh and a woman who had turned out to be a hooker she felt…safe…

'Thank you. And, Ethan…?'

'Yes?'

'Thank you for today. For…well, for coming to my rescue again.'

A long moment and then he nodded, his expression unreadable. 'No problem.'

'Ethan?'

'Yes.'

'Can I ask you something?'

Wariness crossed his face and left behind a guarded expression. 'You can ask…'

'Why did you call me to an interview?'

Silence yawned and Ruby's breath caught. Foolish hope that he had wanted to make amends for the past unfurled.

'Everyone is entitled to a chance,' he said finally. 'And everyone deserves a second one.'

The words were a deep rumble, and fraught with a connotation she couldn't grasp.

'Sleep well, Ruby. We've got a lot of work ahead.'

The door clicked shut behind him and Ruby sank down onto the bed.

Enough. Don't analyse. Don't think. Don't be attracted to him. In other words, don't repeat the mistakes of the past.

Ethan Caversham had offered her a chance and she wouldn't let the jerk of attraction mess that up. Wouldn't kid herself that it was more than that—more like a bond between them. Ruby shook her head—this was an aftermath...an echo of her ancient crush on the man. Because he'd rescued her again.

Only this time it had to play out differently. Instead of allowing the development of pointless feelings and imaginary emotional connections she would concentrate on the job at hand. Get through the trial period, secure the job as a permanent post and then she would be back on track. Heading towards her goal of a family.

One week later

Ethan gave a perfunctory knock and pushed the door open. Ruby looked up from her paper-strewn makeshift desk in the box room where she'd set up office. His conscience panged at her pale face and the dark smudges under her eyes. She'd worked her guts out these past days and he'd let her. More than that—he'd encouraged it.

Get a grip, Ethan.

That was what he paid her to do—to work and work hard. He had high expectations of all his employees and made no bones about it. Ruby was no different.

Sure. Keep telling yourself that, Ethan. Say it enough times and maybe it will become true.

'Earth to Ethan. I was about to call you with an update. I've got delivery dates for the furniture for the banqueting hall and I've found a mural painter. I've mocked up some possible uniforms—black and red as a theme—and…'

'That's all sounds great, but that's not why I'm here. There's something else I need you to do.'

'Okay. No problem. Shoot.'

'Rafael Martinez is coming for dinner and I need you to rustle us up a meal.'

Her dark eyebrows rose. 'Rafael Martinez—billionaire wine guru, owner of the vineyard of all vineyards—is coming for dinner? Why on earth didn't you mention it before?'

'Because I didn't know. I'd scheduled to meet him later this month, but he called to say he's in the UK and that tonight would suit him. I realise it's not ideal. But Rafael and I are...'

Old friends? Nope. Acquaintances? More than that. Old schoolmates? The idea was almost laughable—he and Rafael had bunked off more school than they had attended.

'We go back a while.'

'Maybe you should take him out somewhere?'

'I'd rather discuss business in private. But if it's too much for you...?'

He made no attempt to disguise the challenge in his tone, and she made no attempt to pretend she didn't hear it, angling her chin somewhere between determination and defiance.

'Leave it with me.'

'You're sure?'

'I'm sure.'

'Look on this as a test of your ability to handle a restaurant crisis.'

'Yippee. An opportunity!'

A snort of laughter escaped his lips. 'That's the attitude. I'll leave you to it.'

Whilst he figured out the best way to approach Rafael with his proposition... Rafael Martinez was known more for his playboy tendencies and utterly ruthless business tactics than his philanthropic traits. But Ethan had been upfront in his preliminary approach—had intimated that his agenda was a business deal with a charitable bent—and Rafael had agreed to meet. Somehow it seemed unlikely that he'd done so to reminisce over the bad old days of their more than misguided youth.

He'd reached the doorway when he heard Ruby's voice. 'Actually…I've had an idea…'

Ethan turned. 'Go ahead.'

'Okay. So it's best if you eat in the bar—it's a pretty impressive room, and I think we should make it a little bit Christmassy.'

'Christmassy?' Somehow the idea of Christmas and Rafael didn't exactly gel. 'I don't think so, Ruby. My guess is that Rafael is even less enamoured with the schmaltz of Christmas than me.'

A shake of her dark head and an exaggerated sigh. 'I'm not suggesting schmaltz. If we were open we would be playing the Christmas card—of course we would.' For a second a hint of wistfulness touched her face. 'Can't you picture it? An enormous tree. Garlands. Twinkling lights—' She broke off and frowned. 'I assume all your other business ventures offer Christmas deals and a proper Christmas ambience?'

'Yes, but I don't do it myself.'

He wouldn't have the first clue how—he hadn't celebrated Christmas Day in the traditional sense since...since Tanya was alive.

For a second he was transported back to childhood. His sister had loved Christmas...had made it magical—she had made him help her make paper chains and decorate the tree, and although he'd protested they'd both known the protest to be half-hearted. She'd chivvied their mum into the festive spirit and the day had always been happy. But after Tanya... Well, best not to go there.

'To be honest, I'm not much of a Christmas type of guy. And I'm pretty sure Rafael isn't either.'

'Well, luckily for you I'm a Christmas type of gal. I'm thinking a tasteful acknowledgement of the time of year so that Rafael Martinez gets an idea of how Caversham Castle would showcase his wine. The Martinez Vineyards offer plenty of Christmas wines. Plus, if we do it right the whole Christmas edge might soften him up.'

Difficult to imagine, but given he hoped to appeal to Rafael's charitable side maybe it was worth

a shot. And he believed in encouraging staff ini-
tiative and drive.

'Knock yourself out,' he said.

'Fabulous. I'll hit the shops.'

Ruby crouched down and carefully moved the
small potted tree a couple of centimetres to the left
of the hearth. She inhaled the scent of fir and soil
and felt a small glow of satisfaction at a job well
done. Or at least *she* thought so—Ethan clearly
had reservations about the whole Christmas idea,
and her research into Rafael Martinez had shown
her why.

Like Ethan Caversham, he had a reputation for
ruthlessness, and an internet trawl had revealed
images of a man with a dark aura. Midnight hair,
tall, with a dominant nose and deep black eyes.
Unlike Ethan, he'd left a score of girlfriends in
his wake—all glamorous, gorgeous and very, very
temporary. For a second Ruby dwelled on Ethan,
and curiosity about his love-life bubbled. But it
was none of her business.

He's your boss, nothing more.

'Hey.'

Ruby leapt up and swivelled round. *Chill, Ruby.*

Ethan was many things, but he was not a mind-reader.

'Hey. Sorry. You startled me.' She gestured around. 'What do you think? I was just making sure the trees don't overshadow Dash and Dot.'

'Dash and Dot?'

Ruby chewed her bottom lip. *Idiot.*

Ethan's lips turned up in a sudden small smile and her toes curled. For a second he'd looked way younger, and she could remember her flash of gratification at winning a rare smile all those years ago.

'You named the china dogs?'

'Yes. In my head. I have to admit I didn't intend to share that fact with anyone. But, yes, I did. Queen Victoria had a spaniel called Dash, you see.' Ruby puffed out a sigh. 'And then I thought of Dot because of Morse code. Anyway, what do you think?'

'Excellent names,' he said, his features schooled to gravity, though amusement glinted in his eyes.

Ruby couldn't help but chuckle, despite the clawing worry that he'd loathe what she'd done. 'I meant the decorations.'

Hope that he'd approve mixed with annoyance at her need for approval. A hangover from childhood, when approval had been at high premium and in short supply.

Surely he had to like it? Her gaze swept over the small potted trees on either side of the fireplace and the wreath hanging above. Took in the lightly scented candles on the mantelpiece and the backdrop of tasteful branch lights casting a festive hint.

'It's incredible.'

'No need to sound surprised.' Sheer relief curved her lips into a no doubt goofy grin. 'Admit it. You thought I would produce something ghastly and flashy.'

'I should have had more faith.'

'Absolutely. Don't get me wrong, I can do tacky schmaltz—in fact I have done. A few years back I worked in a café called Yvette's. Yvette herself was lovely, but she was incredibly sentimental. On Valentine's Day you could barely move for helium-filled heart balloons, and as for Christmas... I provided gaudy tinsel, baubles, mistletoe—and this absolutely incredibly tacky light-up Father Christmas that had to be seen to be believed.'

Ethan glanced at her. 'You're a woman of many talents. But what about you? What kind of Christmas is *your* kind?'

The question caught her off guard and without permission her brain conjured up her game plan Christmas. 'Me? Um… Well… I've spent every Christmas working for the past decade, so I go with my employers' flow.'

'So it's just another day for you? You said you were a Christmas kind of gal.'

'I am.' His words pushed all her buttons and she twisted to face him. 'It's a time of celebration. I'm not overly religious, but I do believe it is way more than just another day. It's a time for giving—a magical day.'

His lips were a straight line as he contemplated her words. 'Giving, yes. Magic, no. That's idealistic. Christmas Day doesn't magically put an end to poverty or disease or crime.'

'No, it doesn't. But it is an opportunity to strive for a ceasefire—to try and alleviate sadness and spread some happiness and cheer. Don't you believe that?'

He hesitated, opened his mouth and then closed it again. Waited a beat and then, 'Yes, Ruby. I do believe that.'

'Good. It's also about being with the people you care about and…'

The familiar tug of loss thudded behind her ribcage…the wondering as to the whereabouts of her siblings, the hope that their Christmas would be a joyful one. It would. Of course it would. They had a loving adoptive family, and the thought encased her in a genuine blanket of happiness.

Seeing Ethan's blue-grey eyes resting on her expression, she went on. 'And if you can't do that then I think it's still wonderful to be part of someone else's happiness. That's why I've always worked Christmas Day; watching other families celebrate is enough for now.'

'For now?'

'Sure.' *Keep it light.* 'One day I'll have a family, and then…'

'Then all will be well in the world?' His scathing tone shocked her.

'Yes.' The affirmation fell from her lips with way too much emphasis. 'And when I have a family I can tell you the exact Christmas I'll have. An enormous tree, the scent of pine, crackers, decorated walls, holly, ivy, stockings with a candy cane peering over the top. The table laid with cutlery that gleams in the twinkle of Christmas lights. In the centre a golden turkey and all the extras. Pigs in blankets, roast potatoes, roast parsnips, stuffing and lashings of gravy. But most important of all there'll be children. My family. Because *that* is what Christmas is about. And that is magical.'

Ruby hauled in breath as realisation dawned that she might have got a tad carried away.

'Anyway, obviously that is in the far distant future and not something I need to worry about right now.'

It would take time to save enough money to support a family—time to go through the lengthy adoption process.

'No, it isn't.' Ethan's voice was neutral now, his eyes hooded. 'And now isn't the time to dream of future Christmases.'

'It's not a dream. It's a goal. That's different.'

Dreams were insubstantial clouds—stupid aspirations that might never be attained. Goals—goals were different. Goals were definitive. And Ruby was definite that she would have a family. By hook or by crook.

'But you're right. I need to be in the kitchen—or you and Rafael will be eating candle wax for dinner.'

'Hang on.' His forehead was slashed with a deep frown. 'I meant now is the time to think about present-day Christmas. What are your plans for this year?'

His voice had a rough edge of concern to it and Ruby frowned. The last thing she wanted was for Ethan Caversham to feel sorry for her—the idea was insupportable.

'I'll be fine. I have plans.'

Sure. Her plan was to shut herself away in her apartment and watch weepy movies with a vat of ice cream. But that counted as a plan, right? It wasn't even that she was mourning Hugh—she was bereft at the loss of a dream. Because for all her lofty words she had been stupid enough to take her eye off the goal and allow herself to dream. And Hugh had crushed that dream and trampled it into the dust. Further proof—as if she'd needed it—that dreams were for idiots. Lesson learnt. *Again.* But this time reinforced in steel.

'But thank you for asking.'

Ethan's eyes bored into her and the conviction that he would ask her to expand on the exact nature of her plans opened her lips in pre-emptive strike.

'What about your plans?'

His expression retreated to neutral. 'They aren't firmed up as yet.'

Obscure irrational hurt touched her that he didn't

feel able to share his plans with her. Daft! After all, it wasn't as if she was sharing hers with him.

'Well, I hope they sort themselves out. Right now I must go and cook. Prepare to be amazed!'

CHAPTER FOUR

ETHAN HANDED RAFAEL a crystal tumbler of malt whisky, checked the fire and sat down in the opposite armchair.

Rafael cradled the glass. 'So, my old friend, tell me what it is you want of me?'

'To negotiate a wine deal. You provide my restaurants worldwide at a cost we negotiate. All except here at Caversham Castle—here I'd like you to donate the wine.'

'And why would I do that?' Rafael scanned the room and the slight upturn of his lips glinted with amusement. 'In the spirit of Christmas?'

'Yes,' Ethan said. 'If by that you mean the spirit of giving and caring. Because I plan to run Caversham Castle differently from my other businesses. As a charitable concern. The castle will be open to holidaymakers for nine months of the year and for the remaining three it will be used as a place to help disadvantaged youngsters.'

For a second, the image of him and Rafael, side

by side as they faced down one of the gangs that had roved their estate, flashed in his mind. They had both been loners, but when Rafael had seen him in trouble he'd come to his aid.

'I plan to provide sporting holidays and job-training opportunities. Run fundraisers where they can help out and help organise them. Get involved. Make a difference.' He met Rafael's gaze. 'Give them a chance to do what we've both done.'

After all, they had both been experts in petty crime, headed towards worse, but they had both turned their lives around.

'We did it on our own.'

'Doesn't mean we shouldn't help others.'

Before Rafael could reply the door swung open and Ruby entered.

Whoa. She looked stunning, and Ethan nearly inhaled his mouthful of whisky. Her dark luxuriant hair was swept up in an elegant chignon, clipped with a red barrette. A black dress that reached mid-thigh was cinched at the waist with a wide red sash, and—heaven help him—she wore black peeptoe shoes with jaunty red bows at the heels. Clearly she was giving the new uniform an airing.

A small smile curved her lips as she glided towards them and placed a tray on the table. 'Appetisers to go with your pre-dinner drinks,' she said. 'Parma ham and mozzarella bites, and smoked salmon on crushed potato'.

'Thank you, Ruby.' Attempting to gather his scattered brain cells, Ethan rose to his feet and Rafael followed suit, his dark eyes alight with interest.

'Rafael, this is Ruby Hampton—my restaurant manager.'

'Enchanted to meet you.' Rafael smiled. 'The lady who knocked me off the celebrity gossip pages.'

Colour leached from her face and Ethan stepped towards her.

'I...I hope you enjoyed the respite,' she said, her smile not wavering, and admiration touched his chest. 'I'm not planning on a repeat run.'

Rafael gave a small laugh. 'Well said.' He reached down and picked up one of the canapés and popped it into his mouth. 'Exquisite.'

'Thank you. I'll leave you to it, and then I'll be back with the starters in about fifteen minutes.'

'So...' Rafael said as the door swung shut. 'You've hired Ruby Hampton?'

'Yes.'

'Why? Because you want to give her a second chance?' Rafael gestured round the bar. 'That's what this is about, right? You want people to be given a chance?'

'Yes. I do. I want youngsters who've had a tough time in life to see there is a choice apart from a life of truancy and mindless crime.'

Images of the bleak landscape of the council estate they'd grown up on streamed in his mind.

'And I want society to recognise that they deserve a chance even if they've messed up.'

Rafael leant back. 'You see, *I* think people should make their own choices and prove they deserve a chance. So let's talk business, my friend, and let me think about the charitable angle.'

'Done.'

Ethan placed his whisky glass down. Time to show Rafael Martinez that he might have a philanthropic side, but it didn't mean he wasn't hard-nosed at the negotiating table—helped by the fact that said table was soon occupied by melt-in-the-mouth food, discreetly delivered and served.

In fact if it wasn't for the ultra-sensitive 'detecting Ruby' antennae he seemed to have developed he doubted he would have noticed her presence.

Once the dessert plates were cleared away Ethan

scribbled some final figures down and handed them across to Rafael. 'So we're agreed?'

'We're agreed. I'll get it drawn up legally and the contracts across to you tomorrow.'

'And the wine for Caversham Castle?'

Rafael crossed one long leg across his knee and steepled his fingers together as Ruby entered with a tray of coffee.

'Ruby, I'd like to thank you. Dinner was superb. Why don't you join us for coffee?' His smile widened and Ruby hesitated, but then Rafael rose and pulled out a chair for her. 'I insist. I'm sure you and I will have some contact in the future.'

Half an hour later Ethan resisted the urge to applaud. Conversation had flowed and Ethan could only admire the fact that somehow Ruby had found the time to research Rafael sufficiently to engage him on topics that interested him.

Eventually Ruby rose to her feet and held a hand out to Rafael. 'It's been a pleasure—and now I'll leave you two to get back to business.'

Ruby stood in the gleaming chrome confines of the state-of-the-art kitchens and allowed one puff of weariness to escape her lips as she wiped down the final surface.

Tired didn't cover it—she was teetering on the cliff of exhaustion. But she welcomed it. The past week had been incredible. Sure, Ethan was a hard taskmaster, but the man was a human dynamo—and it had energised her. There were times when she could almost believe the whole debacle with Hugh Farlane had been a bad dream. The only whisper of worry was that it wasn't the work that provided balm—it was working with Ethan.

As if her thoughts had the art of conjure, the kitchen door swung open and there he stood. Still suited in the charcoal-grey wool that fitted him to perfection, he'd shed his tie and undone the top button of the crisp white shirt. Her gaze snagged on the triangle of golden bare skin and her breath caught in her throat as he strode towards her.

Cool it, Ruby.

Will power forced the tumult of her pulse to slow. 'All signed on the dotted line?'

'Yes.' His eyes were alight with satisfaction and she could feel energy vibrate off him. 'Rafael just left and I've come to thank you.'

'No problem. Just doing my job.'

'No. You went the extra mile and then some. The meal, the décor…and then you—you charmed the pants off him.'

His words caused a flinch that she tried to turn into another swipe of the counter; panic lashed her as she reviewed their coffee conversation.

'What's wrong?'

She shrugged and straightened up. 'I guess I'm hoping Rafael didn't think that was my aim in the literal sense.'

Comprehension dawned in his eyes. 'He didn't. You did your job. You liaised.'

His matter-of-fact assurance warmed her very soul. 'Thank you for seeing that. Problem is, I'm not sure everyone will. The world believes I trapped Hugh whilst *liaising* on the job.'

He stepped towards her, frustration evident in the power of his stride, in the tension that tautened his body. 'Then deny the allegations.'

'I can't.'

'Why not? Unless you do feel guilty?' Blue-grey eyes bored into her. 'If he dazzled you with his wealth and charm that doesn't make you a gold-digger. When you start out with nothing it's easy to be swept off your feet—to welcome the idea of lifelong security and easy wealth. There is no need for guilt.'

'I wasn't dazzled by his wealth. I always vowed that I would earn my keep every step of the way.'

Wouldn't set foot on her parents' path. 'I wasn't after Hugh's cash.'

And yet…

A small hard lump of honesty formed in her tummy. 'But I suppose with hindsight I am worried that I was dazzled by the idea of a family. He said he wanted kids, and…'

Yes, there had been that idea of it being within her grasp—the idea that she'd finally found a man who wanted a family. Not a man like Steve or Gary but a man who could provide, who needed her and wanted her help to heal him… What a sucker she'd been. Never again—that was for sure.

'I assume he lied? Like he's lying now? That is his bad. Not yours. So fight him. I had you down as a fighter.'

'I can't win this fight. Hugh Farlane is too big to take on. It's unbelievable how much clout he has. He has enough money to sink a ship…enough publicity people to spin the Bayeux Tapestry.'

'What about right and wrong?'

'That's subjective.'

It was a lesson she had learnt the hard way. She'd fought the good fight before and lost her siblings. Lord knew she was so very happy for them—joyful that Tom and Edie and Philippa had found an adoptive family to love them all. But it had been hard to accept that they would never be the happy family unit she had always dreamed they would be.

So many dreams…woven, threaded, embroidered with intricate care. Of parents who cleaned up their alcohol and drug-fuelled life and transformed themselves into people who cared and nurtured and loved… And when that dream had dissolved she had rethreaded the loom with rose threads and produced a new picture. An adoptive family who would take them all in and provide a normal life—a place where love abounded along with food, drink, clothes and happiness…

She'd fought for both those dreams and been beaten both times. Still had the bruises. So she might have learnt the hard way, but she'd sucked the lesson right up.

'Yes, it is.' His voice was hard. 'But you should still fight injustice. You owe it yourself.'

'No! What I owe myself is to not let my life be wiped out.' *Again*. 'I've worked hard to get where I am now, and I will not throw it away.'

'I don't see how denying these allegations equates to chucking your life away. Unless…'

A deep slash creased his brow and she could

almost hear the cogs of his brain click into gear. For a crazy moment she considered breaking into a dance to distract him. But then…

'Has he forced you to silence? Threatened you?'

Ethan started to pace, his strides covering the resin floor from the grill station with its burnished charbroiler to the sauté station where she stood.

'Is that why you aren't fighting this? Why you haven't refuted the rubbish in the papers? Why Farlane knows he can slate you with impunity and guarantee he'll come up drenched in the scent of roses.'

Just freaking fabulous—he'd worked it out. 'Leave it, Ethan. It doesn't matter. This is my choice. To not add more logs to already fiery flames.'

His expulsion of breath tinged the air with impatience. 'That's a pretty crummy choice.'

'Easy for you to say. You're the multimillionaire head of a global business and best mates with the Rafael Martinezes of the world.'

'That is irrelevant. I would take Hugh Farlane down, whatever my bank balance and connections, because he is a bully. The kind of man who uses his power to hurt and terrorise others.'

Ruby blinked; the ice in his voice had caused the hairs on her arms to stand to attention.

'If you don't stand up to him he will do this to someone else. Bully them, harass them, scare them.'

'No, he won't.'

'You don't know that.'

'Yes, I do...'

Ruby hesitated, tried to tell herself that common sense dictated she end this exchange here and now. But, she couldn't. Her tummy churned in repudiation of the disappointment in his gaze, the flick of disdain in his tone.

'The whole engagement was a set-up.'

The taste of mortification was bitter on her tongue as the words were blurted out.

Ethan frowned. You two were faking a relationship?'

'No. *We* weren't faking. Hugh was. It was a publicity stunt—he needed an urgent image-change. His public were disenchanted with his womanising and his sex addiction. Hugh was keen to get into the more serious side of acting as well, and he wanted to impress the Forsythe sisters, who are notorious for their high moral standards. So he figured he'd get engaged to someone "normal". I fell for it. Hook line and sinker.'

His jaw clenched. 'So it was a scam?'

'Yup. I thought he loved me—in reality he was using me.'

Story of her life.

'I resigned because he asked me to—so that I could be by his side. He told me it was to help him. To keep him from the temptation to stray. But really it was all about the publicity. I can't believe I didn't see it. Hugh Farlane...rich, famous...a man who could have any woman he wanted...decided to sweep *me* off my feet, to change his whole lifestyle, marry me. He said we would live happily ever after with lots of sproglets.' She shook her head. 'I of all people should have known the stupidity of believing *that*.'

Her own parents hadn't loved her enough to change their lifestyles—despite their endless promises to quit, their addictions had held sway over their world. Rendered them immoral and uncaring of anything except the whereabouts of their next fix.

'How did you find out?'

Ethan's voice pulled her back to the present.

'He "confessed" when I found him in bed with

another woman. A hooker, no less. Turned out he'd been sleeping around the whole time. He'd told me that he wanted to wait to sleep with me until we got married, to prove I was "different".'

Little wonder her cheeks were burning—she'd accepted Hugh's declaration as further evidence of his feelings for her, of his willingness to change his lifestyle for her, and her soul had sung.

'In reality it was so that he could be free at night for some extracurricular action between the sheets.'

For a second a flicker of relief crossed his face, before sheer contempt hardened his features to granite. Both emotions she fully grasped. If she'd actually slept with Hugh she would feel even more besmirched than she already did. As for contempt—she'd been through every shade, though each one had been tinted with a healthy dose of self-castigation at her own stupidity.

'Anyway, once I got over the shock I chucked the ring at him, advised him to pay the woman with it and left. Then his publicity machine swung into action. Hugh's first gambit was to apologise. It was cringeworthy. Next up, ironically enough, he offered to pay me to play the role of his fiancée. When I refused, it all got a bit ugly.'

Ethan halted, his jaw and hands clenched. 'You want me to go and find him? Drag him here and make him grovel?'

'No!'

But his words had loosed a thrill into her veins—there was no doubt in her mind that he would do exactly that. For a second she lingered on the satisfying image of a kowtowing Hugh Farlane and she gave a sudden gurgle of laughter.

'I appreciate it, but no—thank you. The point is he said he'd never bother to pull a publicity stunt like this again. So I don't need to make a stand for the greater good. To be honest, I just want it to blow over; I want the threats and the hatred to stop.'

Ethan drummed his fingers on the counter and her flesh goosebumped at his proximity, at the level of anger that buzzed off him. It was an anger with a depth that filled her with the urge to try to soothe him. Instinct told her this went deeper than outrage on her behalf, and her hand rose to reach out and touch him. Rested on his forearm.

His muscles tensed and his blue-grey gaze contemplated her touch for a stretch. Then he covered her hand with his own and the sheer warmth made her sway.

'I'm sorry you went through that, Ruby. I'd like to make the bastard pay.'

'It's okay.' Ruby shook her head. 'I'm good. Thanks to you. You gave me a chance, believed in me, and that means the world.'

Lighten the mood. Before you do something nuts like lean over and kiss him on the cheek. Or just inhale his woodsy aroma.

'If it weren't for you I'd still be under my duvet, ice cream in hand. Instead I'm here. Helping renovate a castle. So I'm really good, and I want to move forward with my life.'

'Then let's do exactly that.' Ethan nodded. 'Let's go to dinner.'

'Huh?' Confusion flicked her, along with a thread of apprehension at the glint in his eye. 'Now? You've had dinner, remember?'

'Tomorrow. Pugliano's. In the next town along.'

'Pugliano's? You're kidding? We'd never get in at such short notice.'

'Don't worry about that. We'll get a table.'

'But why do you want us to go out for dinner?' For a scant nanosecond her heart speeded up, made giddy by the idea that it was a date.

'To celebrate making your appointment official. You're off trial.'

'I am?' A momentary emotion she refused to acknowledge as disappointment that it was not a date twanged. To be succeeded by suspicion. 'Why?'

Shut up, shut up, shut up.

This was good news, right? The type that should have her cartwheeling around the room. But...

'I don't want this job out of pity.'

'Look at me.' He met her gaze. 'Do I look like a man who would appoint someone to an important business role out of pity?'

'Fair point. No, you don't. But I think your timing is suspect.'

'Nope. You've proved yourself this past week. You've matched my work drive without complaint and with enthusiasm. Tonight you went beyond the call of duty with Rafael and now you've told me the truth. No pity involved. So... Dinner?'

'Dinner.'

Try as she might the idea sizzled—right alongside his touch. His hand still covered hers and she wanted more.

As if realisation hit him at the same instant he released his grip and stepped backwards. 'It will be good for you as well. To see how Pugliano's works.'

'Good…how?' Hurt flickered across her chest. 'I've researched all your places. I've talked to your restaurant managers in Spain and France and New York. Plus I know how a top-notch restaurant works already.'

'Sure—but as a manager, not as a guest.' He raised a hand. 'I know your engagement to Hugh was filled with social occasions in glitzy places, but you said it yourself you didn't enjoy them and now I get why. I want you to see it from the point of view of a guest. Experience it from *that* side of the table.'

Despite all her endeavour, the bit of her that persisted in believing the date scenario pointed out that she would positively *revel* in the experience alongside Ethan.

The thought unleashed a flutter of apprehension. *Chill, Ruby. And think this through.*

This was *not* a date, and actually… 'I'm not sure it's a good idea. What if it reactivates the media hype? What if people think that I'm moving in on *you*, shovel in hand, kitted out in my gold-prospecting ensemble?'

His broad shoulders shrugged with an indifference she could only envy. 'Does it matter what people think?'

'It does if it starts up a media storm.'

'We can weather the storm. This is a business dinner, not a date, and I don't have a problem going public with that.'

'Well, *I* do. I can picture it—sitting there being stared at, whispered about…the salacious glances…'

'But once they see two people clearly in the process of having a business dinner they will lose interest and stop gawping.'

'What about the negative publicity viewpoint?'

'You are my *restaurant manager*. You do your job and I will deal with any negative publicity. I stand by my employees. Look, I get that it will be hard, but if you want to move on you need to face it. I'll be right there by your side.'

'I get that it will be hard… You need to face it… I'll be right there by your side.'

The phrases echoed along the passage of a decade—the self-same words that the younger Ethan Caversham had uttered.

Those grey-blue eyes had held her mesmerised and his voice, his sheer presence, had held her panic attacks at bay. It had been Ethan who had made her leave the hostel, who had built her confidence so she could walk the streets again, only this time with more assurance, with a poise engendered by the self-defence classes he'd enrolled her in.

Yes—for weeks he'd been by her side. Then he'd gone. One overstep on her part, one outburst on his, and he'd gone. Left her. Moved out and away, leaving no forwarding address.

Ruby met his gaze, hooded now, and wondered if he had travelled the same memory route. She reminded herself that now it was different—*she* was different. No way would she open herself to that hurt again—that particular door was permanently closed and armour-plated.

So Ethan was right—to move forward she needed to put herself out there.

'Let's do this.'

CHAPTER FIVE

ETHAN RESISTED THE urge to loosen his collar as he waited in front of the limo outside the castle's grand entrance. This strange fizz of anticipation in his gut was not acceptable—not something he'd experienced before, and not something he wanted to experience again.

Fact One: this was *not* a date. A whoosh of irritation escaped his lips that he needed a reminder of the obvious. The word date was not in Ethan Caversham's dictionary.

Fact Two: Ruby was an *employee* and this was a business dinner, to give her a guest's viewpoint and to show her—an *employee*—his appreciation of a job well done. Perhaps if he stressed the word *employee* enough his body and mind would grasp the concept…

Fact Three: yes, they had a shared past—but that past consisted of a brief snapshot in time, and that tiny percentage of time was not relevant to the present.

So… Those were the facts and now he was sorted. De-fizzed. Ethan Caversham was back in control.

A minute later the front door opened and every bit of his control was blown sky-high, splattering him with the smithereens of perspective. Moisture sheened his neck as he slammed his hands into his pockets and forced himself not to rock back on his heels.

Ruby looked sensational, and all his senses reeled in response. Her glorious dark hair tumbled loose in glossy ripples over the creamy bare skin of her shoulders. The black lacy bodice of her dress tantalised his vision. A wide black band emphasised the slender curve of her waist and the dress was ruched into a fun, flirty skirt that showcased the length of her legs.

But what robbed his lungs of breath was the expression on her face and the very slight question in her sapphire eyes. That hint of masked vulnerability smote him with a direct jab to the chest.

'You look stunning.'

'Thank you.' Her chin angled in defiance. 'I decided that if people are going to stare I'd better scrub up.'

'You scrub up well.'

With a gargantuan effort he kept his tone light, pushed away the urge to pull her into his arms and show her how well, to try to soothe the apprehension that pulsed from her.

'Your limo awaits.'

'You didn't need to hire a limo.'

'I wanted to. We're celebrating, and I want to do this in style—tonight I want you to enjoy the experience of being a guest.'

To make up in some small way for what Hugh had put her through. All those high society occasions where he'd groomed her to act a part she'd disliked. Sheer anger at the actor's behaviour still fuelled Ethan—to have messed with Ruby's head like that was unforgivable. So tonight it was all about Ruby. As his *employee.* His temple pounded a warning—perspective needed to be retained.

'So that you can use the experience to help you at Caversham Castle. Speaking of which…I've issued a press statement.'

'Good idea.' The words were alight with false brightness as she slid into the limousine. Waited for him to join her in sleek leather luxury. 'What did it say?'

'"Ethan Caversham is pleased to announce the appointment of a restaurant manager for his new project, Caversham Castle in Cornwall. Ruby Hampton has taken on the role, and both Ethan and Ruby are excited at the prospect of creating a restaurant that sparkles with all the usual Caversham glitter and offers a dining experience to savour.'"

'Sounds good.'

After that, silence fell, and Ethan forced his gaze away from her beauty and instead gazed out at the scenery. A quick glance at Ruby saw her doing the same. There was tension in the taut stance of her body and in the twisting of her hands in her lap.

'You okay?' he asked.

'Sure.' The word was too swift, the smile too bright.

'It's all right to be nervous. You've been in hiding for weeks.'

'I'll be fine.' Slim bare shoulders lifted. 'I just loathe being gawped at. You know…? Plus, you *do* realise there is every chance people will chuck bread rolls at me, or worse?'

'Not on my watch,' he said as the limo glided to a stop. 'But if they do we'll face it together.' The words were all wrong. 'As employer and employee—colleagues…professionals.' Okay… Now he was overcompensating. 'You can do this, Ruby.'

A small determined nod was her response as the car door was opened by the driver. Ethan slid along the leather seat and stepped out, waited as Ruby followed suit. Before she could so much as step from the car a bevy of reporters flocked around them. Quelling the urge to actually move closer to her, Ethan turned to face them, angled his body to shield Ruby.

'So, Ruby, have you decided to break your silence about Hugh Farlane?'

'Ethan, is it true that you've *hired* Ruby, or is this something more personal?'

Ethan raised his hands. 'Easy, guys. Give Ruby some space, please. We get that you're pleased to see her, but she needs to breathe. I need my new restaurant manager to be fully functional.'

Next to him, he sensed the shudder of tension ripple through her body, heard her inhalation of breath—and then she stepped forward.

'Hey, guys. I'm happy to chat about my new role—which I am *very* excited about as the next step in my career—but I have nothing to say about Hugh.'

His chest warmed with admiration at the cool confidence of her tone and the poise she generated.

'That's old news,' he interpolated. 'Our concern is with the future and with Caversham's new venture. Ruby is already doing an amazing job, and I'm looking forward to continuing to work with her.'

'Best keep an eye on your wallet, then, Ethan!'

'What about you, Ruby? Is this a new game plan? To get your mitts on Ethan and the Caversham bank balance?'

She flinched, and Ethan swivelled with lethal speed, the urge to lash out contained and leashed, his tone smooth as ice.

'My wallet is perfectly safe, but many thanks for your concern. I have no doubt that Ruby has the same game plan as me. Right now I'm concentrating on the grand opening of Caversham Castle—the guest list is shaping up nicely. My plan is to grant exclusive coverage to a magazine—though I haven't decided who yet. Perhaps we'll discuss it over dinner.'

The implication was clear. *Drop the gold-digger angle and you might be in with a chance.*

The reporters dispersed, oiled away with ingratiating smiles, and satisfaction touched him.

They would stop ripping Ruby to shreds, Hugh Farlane would in turn back off, public interest would die down and the bullies and the nutcases would retreat.

His aim was achieved—his anger channelled to achieve the desired result. Control was key—emotions needed to be ruled and used. When you let your emotions rule you then you lost control. And Ethan was never walking that road again.

Without thought he placed his hand on the small of her back to guide her forward and then wished he hadn't. *Too close, too much*—a reminder that the physical awareness hadn't diminished.

It was with relief that he entered the warmth of the restaurant and Ruby stepped away from him. Her face flushed as her gaze skittered away from his and she looked around.

'Wow!'

'Tony Pugliano is a fan of Christmas,' Ethan said.

The whole restaurant was a dazzling testament to that. The winter grotto theme was delicate, yet pervasive. Lights like icicles glittered from the ceiling and a suspended ice sculpture captured the eye. Windows and mirrors were frosted, and each table displayed scented star-shaped candles that filled the room with the elusive scent of Christmas.

'It's beautiful...' Ruby breathed.

'You like it?' boomed a voice.

Ethan dragged his gaze from Ruby's rapt features to see Tony Pugliano crossing the floor towards them.

'Ethan.' Tony pulled him into a bear hug and slapped his back. 'This is fabulous, no? Welcome to my winter palace. Ruby—it's good to see you.'

'You too—and it's glorious, Tony.'

The grizzled Italian beamed. 'And now, for you, I have reserved the best table—you will be private, and yet you will appreciate every bit of the restaurant's atmosphere. Anything you want you must ask and it is yours, my friends.'

'Thank you, Tony. We appreciate it.'

'We really do,' Ruby said as they followed in Tony's expansive wake to a table that outdid all the other tables in the vicinity.

Crystal glasses seized the light and glittered from each angled facet, a plethora of star candles dotted the table, and the gleam of moisture sheened the champagne already in an ice bucket.

'Sit, sit...' Tony said. 'I have, for you, chosen

the best—the very best of our menu. You need not even have to think—you can simply enjoy.'

Ruby watched his departing back and opened her mouth, closed it again as a waiter glided towards them, poured the champagne and reverently placed a plate of canapés in front of them.

'Made by Signor Pugliano himself. There is *arancini di riso* filled with smoked mozzarella cheese, radicchio ravioli, bresaola and pecorino crostini drizzled with truffle oil, and Jerusalem artichokes with chestnut velouté, perfumed with white truffle oil.'

'That sounds marvellous,' Ruby managed.

Once the waiter had gone she met Ethan's gaze, clocked his smile and forced her toes to remain uncurled. It was a smile—nothing more.

'This is almost as miraculous as what I just witnessed. I am considering how to lift my jaw from my knees.' She shook her head. 'Tony Pugliano is renowned as one of the toughest, most brusque, most temperamental chefs in the country and round you he's turned into some sort of pussycat. How? Why? What gives?'

His smile morphed into a grin. 'It's my famous charm.'

'Rubbish.' However charming Ethan was—and that was a point she had no wish to dwell on—it wouldn't affect Tony Pugliano. 'Plus, I know Hugh eats here, so I'm amazed he seemed so happy to see me.'

'You are underrating my charm capacity,' Ethan said.

Picking up a canapé, she narrowed her eyes. Nope—she wasn't buying it. This was zip to do with charm, but clearly Ethan had no intention of sharing. No surprise there, then.

'Especially given his less than accommodating attitude when I applied for a job here after my break-up with Hugh. Whereas now, if you asked him to, he'd probably give me any job I asked for.' Seeing his eyebrows rise she shook her head. 'Not that I *want* you to do that!'

'You sure?' There was an edge to his voice under the light banter.

Disbelief and hurt mingled. Surely Ethan couldn't possibly think she would go after another job. 'I am one hundred per cent sure. You gave me a chance when no one else would give me the opportunity to wash so much as a dish. So you get one hundred per cent loyalty.'

'I appreciate that.'

Yet the flatness of his tone was in direct variance to the fizz of champagne on her tongue. 'Ethan. I mean it.'

His broad shoulders lifted and for a second the resultant ripple of muscle distracted her. But only for a heartbeat.

'There isn't such a thing as one hundred per cent loyalty. Everyone has a price or a boundary that dissolves loyalty.'

The edge of bitterness caught at her. Had someone let him down? All of a sudden it became imperative that he believed in her.

'Well, *I* don't. You're stuck with me for the duration.'

His large hand cradled his glass, set the light amber liquid swirling. 'If you had an opportunity to have a family then your loyalty might lose some percentage points. Likewise if I stopped paying your salary your allegiance would be forfeit.' He pierced a raviolo. 'That's life, Ruby. No big deal.'

'It is a *huge* deal—and I think I need to make something clear. I do want children, but that does not take precedence above this job. Right now my top priority is to see Caversham Castle firmly ensconced as the lodestar of Caversham Holiday Adventures. I have no intention of starting a family until I am financially secure, with a house, savings in the bank and the ability to support one. But even if I won the Lottery I would not let you down. As for you not paying me—I know you would only do that in a crisis. I would always believe that you'd turn that crisis around, so you'd still have my loyalty.'

Ethan didn't look even remotely moved—it was as if her words had slid off his smooth armour of cynicism.

Dipping a succulent morsel of artichoke into the chestnut velouté, she savoured the taste, wondered how else she could persuade him. She looked up and encountered an ironic glint in his eyes.

'Forget the Lottery. What if Mr Perfect turns up and says he wants a family right now? I wouldn't see you for dust.'

The words stung—what would it take to show him that he could trust her? 'That won't happen because I'm not planning on a meeting with Mr Perfect. I don't *need* Mr Perfect—or Mr Anyone. My plan is to be a single parent.'

His grey-blue eyes hardened, all emotion vanishing to leave only ice.

The advent of their waiter was a relief and a prevention of further conversation. As if sensing the tension, he worked deftly to remove their used plates and replace them.

'Here is langoustine cooked three different ways. Roasted with a hint of chilli and served with puy lentils, grilled with seared avocado and manuka honey, and a langoustine mousseline with manzanilla,' he said swiftly, before making a dignified retreat with a discreet, *'Buon appetito.'*

Ethan didn't so much as peek down at his plate, and Ruby forced herself to hold his gaze even as regret pounded her temples. Of all the idiotic conversational paths to take, telling Ethan about her single parenthood aspirations rated right up there as the Idiot Trail. Her intent had been to prove her loyalty was genuine, to *reassure* him. Which was nuts. Ethan was a billionaire…head of a global business—he did not need reassurance from one restaurant manager minion.

'This looks delicious,' she ventured.

'Enjoy it whilst you can. Single parenthood doesn't offer much opportunity to eat like this.'

Was he for real? A trickle of anger seeped into her veins. 'That's a bit of a sweeping statement, don't you think?'

His snort of derision caused her toes to tingle with the urge to kick him.

'No. Do you have any idea of the reality of single parenthood? How hard it is?'

Swallowing down the threat of a mirthless laugh, she slapped some of the langoustine mousse onto some bread and took a bite. Tried to concentrate on the incredible hit to her tastebuds instead of the memories that hovered before her—memories of those childhood years when she had effectively looked after her siblings. Dark-haired Tom, blue-eyed Philippa and baby Edie…

Yes! she wanted to shout. Yes, she did know how hard it was—but she also knew with all her being that it was worth it.

'I fully understand how enormous a responsibility parenting is and I know it will be hard. But I also know it will be incredibly rewarding.'

Ever since she'd lost her siblings, understood she would never be with them again. Ruby had known with every cell of her body and soul that she wanted a family.

Desperately she tried to neutralise her expression but it was too late—his blue-grey eyes considered her and his face lost some of its scowl.

'Those are words, Ruby. Easy to say. But the reality of caring for a family and supporting them at the same time on your own is way more daunting.' His voice sounded less harsh, yet the words were leaden with knowledge.

'I know it won't be easy.'

'No, it won't. Plus it's not all about babies and how cute and sweet they are.'

'I get that.' Her teeth were now clenched so tightly her jaw ached. 'I am not a fool, basing a decision like this on a baby's cute factor.'

Given her plan to adopt, it was more than possible that she'd opt for older children. Children such as she and her siblings had been.

'Babies grow up—into toddlers, into schoolchildren and into teenagers. Sometimes when you're on your own, trying to do it all, it can go wrong.' A shadow darkened his features and he scoured his palm over his face as if in an effort to erase it.

For a heartbeat doubt shook her—Tom had been five, the girls even younger when social services had finally hauled the whole family into care. If that hadn't happened would it all have gone wrong for them? Maybe it would—but that was because back then she'd been a child herself. This time she had it all *planned*.

'I told you. I won't embark on having a family until I have sufficient resources to make it possible. I will make sure I can work part-time, I will

have the best childcare known to mankind, and—'
Breaking off, she picked up her fork and pulled
her plate towards her. Shook her head. 'I have
no idea why I am justifying myself to you. Who
made you the authority on single parenthood?'

'No one. But I am concerned that you are jump-
ing the gun. Just because Hugh Farlane turned out
to be a number one schmuck it doesn't mean you
have to dive into single parenthood. Maybe this
desire for kids on your own is a reaction to how
badly it worked out with Hugh. I don't think you
should make any hasty decisions, that's all. It's a
mighty big step to take.'

His deep tone had gentled, the concern in it un-
doubtedly genuine, and that was worse than his
scorn. That she could have dismissed, or coun-
tered with anger. But care triggered in her an
alarming yearn to confide in him, to explain that
her desire for a family was way more than a whim
activated by Hugh's perfidy.

Bad idea. Yet she had to say something.

'I know that.' She did. 'But this is not a rebound
decision from Hugh. Truly it isn't. It feels right.'

'Why?'

Ruby hesitated, picked up her glass and sipped
a swirl of champagne, relieved to see their waiter

approaching. Her brain raced as he placed the next course in front of them, rapidly explained that it consisted of crispy skinned chicken breast with black truffles, spinach and a white port sauce, and then discreetly melted into the background.

This would be the perfect opportunity to turn the conversation. Yet surely there was no harm in answering the question—maybe it was time to remind herself of her goals and her motivations... set it all out.

A warning chime pealed from the alcoves of her mind. This was meant to be a professional dinner. It was hard to see that this conversation was anything *but* personal. But for some indefinable reason it seemed natural. The ding-dong of alarm pealed harder. This was how it had felt a decade before. Curled up in a chair in the beige metallic confines of a hostel room, the temptation to talk and confide had ended up in disaster.

But it was different now, and...and, *truth be told*—she wanted him to know that she was all grown up...not some daft girl who hadn't thought through the idea of going it alone into parenthood. So one last explanation and then she would move the conversation into professional waters.

CHAPTER SIX

ETHAN KNEW THAT the whole discussion had derailed spectacularly and that it behoved him to push it onto a blander path.

But, he couldn't. Intrigue and frustration intermeshed at the idea of Ruby launching herself into the murk of single parenthood through choice.

Chill, Ethan.

There were many, many excellent single parents—he knew that. But it was a tough road; he knew from bitter personal experience exactly how difficult it was—had seen how it had played out for his mother.

'So why single parenthood?' he repeated.

Ruby carefully cut up a piece of chicken and for a moment he thought she would change the subject, then she put her cutlery down and shrugged.

'Because I'm not exactly clued up at choosing good father material.'

'Just because Hugh didn't work out…'

Ruby snorted. '"Didn't work out" is a bit of an

understatement. But the point is that it's not just Hugh. You see, Hugh wasn't the first person to tug the wool over my eyes. Being taken in is my speciality—I could write a thesis. When I was nineteen there was Gary. I believed Gary to be a misunderstood individual who had been wrongfully dismissed. Turned out he was a drunken layabout who'd been quite rightly fired. Then a few years later there was Steve—a self-confessed gambler who swore himself hoarse that he was trying to quit. In reality he was keen on extracting as much money from me as possible to fund the local betting shop.'

A wave of her fork in his direction.

'Hugh you know about. So surely you can see the theme here. I am not a good judge of character. So it makes sense to do this alone.'

'But why do it at all? Or at least why do it now? You're twenty-six.'

'You are thirty. Most thirty-year-olds aren't billionaire CEOs of their own global business. Ten years ago I knew I wanted a family and you knew you wanted to make it big. You've done that through grit and hard work and drive. Well, now I am doing the same to get a family.'

A frown slashed his brow. 'Children aren't an acquisition.'

'I am not suggesting they are.' She gave an expressive roll of her eyes as she huffed out a breath that left her exasperation to hover in the air. '*Sheesh*. What is wrong with wanting to have children?'

'Nothing.'

For Pete's sake—he'd muttered the word, and now his lips had pressed together as a barrier to the further words that wanted to spill from his lips with unprecedented freedom. To stem the explanation that having children could lead to devastation not joy.

His mother had been deprived of her daughter—her pride and joy. For an instant the image of Tanya's lifeless body assaulted his brain. His sister—driven to take her own life. And he hadn't known—hadn't been able to protect her.

His mother had been left with him, her son, a mirror image of her violent criminal husband. The son she had never been able to love but had done her duty by. Until he'd driven her to snap point and she'd washed her hands of him.

For a split second the memory of the packed case and the hand-over to social services jarred his brain. No fault of hers—in her eyes he'd been on the road to following his father's footsteps. His impassioned pleas for forgiveness and promises to reform would have simply been further shades of the man she despised.

Ethan shut down the thought process and concentrated on Ruby's face. Those sapphire eyes, delicate features and that determined chin. Her expression of challenge had morphed into one of concern and he forced his vocal cords into action and his face into neutral.

'There is nothing wrong with wanting children. I just think you need to give single parenthood a lot of thought and not enter the whole venture with rose-coloured spectacles. That's all.'

End of subject, and Ethan picked up his knife and fork and started to eat.

Ruby twirled a tendril of hair around her finger. 'What about you? Where do you stand on the venture into parenthood? Don't you hope for a family one day?'

'No.'

The idea of a family was enough to bring him out in hives. Family had brought him nothing except a one-way channel to loss, heartbreak and rejection. So what was the point?

'Never?' Surprise laced her tone.

'No.' Perhaps monosyllables would indicate to Ruby that this wasn't a topic he wished to pursue.

'Why not?'

Clearly the indirect approach hadn't worked—so it was time to make it clear.

'That's my personal choice.'

Hurt mingled with anger flashed across her features. *Fair enough, Ethan.* He'd been mighty fine with a personal conversation when it was *her* personal life under discussion.

'In brief, it's not what I want. Like you. I've worked hard to get to where I am and I don't want to rock the boat. I'm exactly where I want to be. And I know exactly where I'm going.'

'Isn't that a bit boring? I mean, will that be your life for ever? Buy another property…set up another venture? What happens when you run out of countries?'

Ethan blinked at the barrage of questions. 'Boring? I run a global business, travel the world on a daily basis, have more than enough money and a pretty nifty lifestyle. So, nope. Not humdrum.'

'But…' A shake of her head and she turned her attention back to her plate.

Following suit, he took another mouthful, tried to appreciate the delicacy of the truffles, the infusion of port, the tenderness of the meat. To his own irritation he couldn't let it go.

'But what?'

Her shoulders lifted and for a second his gaze lingered on the creamy skin, the enticing hint of cleavage.

'That world of yours—that non-rocking boat of yours—only contains you, and that sounds lonely. Unless you're in a relationship that you haven't mentioned?'

'Nope. It's a one-man vessel and I'm good with that.'

'So you don't want a long-term relationship or kids? Ever?'

'I don't want any type of relationship. Full stop. I make sure my…my liaisons are brief.' Like a night—a weekend, tops.

Ruby's eyed widened and his exasperation escalated as he identified compassion in her.

'But you've worked so hard to build up Caversham. What's the point if you don't have someone to hand it over to?'

'That's hardly a reason to have a child.'

'Not a reason, but surely part of being a parent is the desire to pass on your values or beliefs. A part of yourself.'

The very idea made him go cold. 'I think that's a bit egocentric. You can't have children just to inculcate them with your beliefs.'

'No!' She shook her head, impatience in the movement. 'You're making it sound as if I want to instil them with questionable propaganda. I don't. But I *do* believe we are programmed with a need to nurture. To love and be loved.'

'Well, I'm the exception to the rule.'

Her chin angled in defiance. 'Or your programming has gone haywire.'

Ethan picked his glass up and sipped the fizz. No way would he rise to that bait.

'The point is, even if you're right, it is wrong to put that burden on someone. That responsibility. You shouldn't have a child just because you want someone to love and love you back. There are enough people out there already. The world doesn't need more.'

'Actually...' Ruby hesitated.

'Actually, what?'

'Nothing.'

Before he could respond the boom of Tony Pugliano's voice rang out. 'So, my friends. It was all to your liking?'

Ruby's thoughts whirled as she strove to concentrate on Tony's question, primed her lips to smile. Maybe this was an intervention from providence itself—a reinforcement of her decision to cease with the confidences.

'It was incredible, Tony!' she stated.

'How could it be anything else?' the chef declared. 'And now we have the perfect end to the perfect meal—I have for you a sample of the very best desserts in the world.'

He waved an expansive hand and the waiter appeared with an enormous platter, which he placed in the middle of the table.

'I, Tony Pugliano, prepared these with my own hands for your delectation. There is praline mousseline with cherry confit, clementine cheesecake, almond and black sesame pannacotta and a dark chilli chocolate lime *torta*.' He beamed as he clapped Ethan on the shoulder. 'And of course all this is on the house.'

There went her jaw again—headed kneewards.

On the house. She doubted such words had ever crossed Tony's lips before.

'You look surprised. No need. Because never, *never* can I thank this man enough. You saved my Carlo—my one and only child. You are a good man, Ethan, and I thank you with all my heart.'

Tony seemed sublimely unaware of Ethan's look of intense discomfort. Yet the shadow in Ethan's eye, the flash of darkness, made her chest band in instinctive sympathy.

'I think this meal goes a long way towards thanks,' she said. 'It was divine. I don't suppose you would share the secret of the truffle sauce in...?'

The tactic worked. As if recalled to his chef persona, Tony gave a mock roar and shook his head.

'*Never.* Not even for you would I reveal the Pugliano family secret. It has passed from one generation to the next for centuries and shall remain sacrosanct for ever. Now—I shall leave you to enjoy the fruit of my unsurpassable skills.'

Once he had made a majestic exit, Ethan nodded. 'Thanks for the change of subject.'

'No problem.' Ruby reached out and selected a mini-dessert. 'I knew it took more than charm to get Tony Pugliano grazing from your hand.

Whatever you did for his son must have been a big deal.'

Ethan shrugged his shoulders, the casual gesture at variance with the wariness in his clenched jaw. 'I was in a position to help his son and I did so. Simple as that.'

'It didn't sound simple to me. More like fundamental.'

'How about another change of subject?'

Picking up a morsel of cheesecake, he popped it in his mouth. His expression was not so much closed as locked, barred *and* padlocked—with a 'Trespassers Will Be Prosecuted' sign up to boot.

'I think our dinner conversation has gone a bit off the business track.'

He wasn't wrong. In fact she should be doused in relief that he didn't want to rewind their conversational spool. Because she had been on the cusp of intimacy—tempted to confide to Ethan that her plan was to adopt, about to spill even more of her guts. And a girl needed her intestines to survive. Something she would do well to remember.

Her family plans were zilch to do with Ethan Caversham. And similarly there was no need for her to wonder why he had decided to eschew love of any sort from a partner or a child. Over the past week she'd gained his trust, they had built up an easy working relationship, and she would not risk that. She mustn't let this man tug her into an emotional vortex again. Ten years ago it had been understandable. Now it would be classed as sheer stupidity.

'So,' he said. 'How about we start with what you think of this restaurant? With your guest's hat on?'

'Modern. Sweeping. The glass effect works to make it sleek, and his table placement is extraordinary. I love the balcony—it's contemporary and it's got buzz. Those enormous flower arrangements are perfect. As for the Christmas effect— it is superb.'

Maybe she could blame the glitter of the pseudo icicles or the scent of cinnamon and gingerbread that lingered in the air for flavouring their conversation with intimacy...

'Definitely five-star. But is this what you want for Caversham?'

'Five stars? Absolutely.'

'I get that, but I have an idea that you're holding some information back. About your plans for the castle.' Something she couldn't quantify made her know that what Tony Pugliano had achieved wasn't exactly what Ethan was after. His body stilled and she scooped up a spoonful of the cheesecake, allowed the cold tang of clementine to melt on her tongue. 'Am I right?'

Ethan drummed a rhythm on the table. 'Yes,' he said finally. 'But it's on a need-to-know basis.'

'Don't you think that as your restaurant manager I "need to know"?'

'Yes—and when it's the right time I will tell you. For now, I'd like to discuss the grand opening.'

Determination not to show hurt allowed her to nod, relieved that the movement shook her hair forward to shield her expression from those all-seeing eyes.

'Fair enough.'

An inhalation of breath and she summoned enthusiasm—she *was* excited about her ideas for the event and she would not let Ethan's caginess shadow that.

'I thought we could have a medieval theme—maybe even a ball. And what do you think about the idea of making it a fundraiser? I know we've already confirmed the guest list, but I think people will happily buy tickets for a good cause. Especially if they also get publicity from it. We could offer exclusive coverage to one of the celebrity gossip mags and—'

Ruby broke off. Ethan sat immobile, his silence uninterpretable.

Then… 'It's a great idea,' Ethan said. A sudden rueful smile tipped his lips and curled her toes. 'In fact it ties in perfectly with my ideas for the castle. So I guess you now "need to know".' His smile vanished and left his lips in a hard straight line. 'In brief, I want to run Caversham Castle as a charitable venture. So kick-starting it with a fundraiser would work well.'

It was as if each word had been wrung from him and confusion creased her brow. 'I love the idea, but can you tell me more? Is it a particular charity you want to raise money for? The more information I have the more successful I can make the event.'

'The money raised will go to a charity that helps troubled teens. Gets them off the streets, helps them back on their feet if they've been in juvie.'

It took a few moments for the true meaning of his words to make an impact, and then it took all her will-power not to launch herself across the table and wrap her arms around him. Only the knowledge that they were in a public place and the suspicion that Ethan would loathe the display kept her in her seat. But the idea that Ethan Caversham, renowned tough guy and entrepreneur, had a different side to him made her tummy go gooey. He'd experienced life on the streets, been a troubled teen himself and now he wanted to help others.

'I think that is an amazing idea. Brilliant. We will make this the best fundraiser ever.' Her mind was already fizzing with ideas. 'How about we go back to my suite for coffee and a brainstorm?'

Ethan bit back a groan and tried to get a grip. Better late than never, after all. Somehow he'd utterly lost his grasp of events—the conversation had spiralled out of control and now he could see more than a flicker of approval in Ruby's eyes. An approval he didn't want.

Time to try and relocate even a shard of perspective.

Ruby was his employee—one who could help make this fundraiser work. Therefore he should be pleased at her enthusiasm and accept her approval on a professional level, not a personal one.

So... 'Coffee and a brainstorm sound good.'

'Perfect.' A blink of hesitation and then she

reached out and covered his hand with her own. 'I will make this *rock*. I remember how it felt to be a teenager on the streets. It was like being shrouded in invisibility. Even the people who dropped a ten pence piece in front of me did it without even a glance.'

A small shiver ran through her body, and her eyes were wide in a face that had been leached of colour.

'The idea of subsisting on people's charity made me feel small and helpless and angry and very alone.'

The image of Ruby huddled on the streets smote his chest.

'It is an endemic problem. I know there are hostels and soup kitchens and the like, and that is incredible, but I want to do something more hands-on, more direct—' He broke off.

The image of a homeless Ruby had set him galloping on his hobby horse.

'Like what?' She leant forward, her entire being absorbed in their conversation. 'Come on, Ethan—spill. I want to help.'

Her sincerity was vibrant and how could he quench that? It would be wrong.

'My idea for the castle is to open it as a luxury

hotel for nine months of the year and then use the proceeds to utilise it differently for the remaining three months. As a place for troubled teens. Surfing holidays but also training courses, so they can learn job skills—maybe in the hotel industry.'

He'd explained his idea to Rafael, but somehow the words were much harder to utter now—maybe because Rafael understood his need for redemption, retribution, second chances. Ruby didn't. And there it was—the dawning of approbation, the foretaste of hero worship simmering in her beautiful eyes.

'That is an awesome idea,' she said quietly. 'Truly. Tony was right. You are a good man.'

The words were not what he wanted to hear—there was too much in his past for him to have earned that epithet.

'I'm not quite ready for a halo—all I plan to do is use the profits from a business venture to try and do some good. That's all. Don't big it up into more than it is.'

A push of the nearly empty dessert plate across the table.

'Now, eat up and then let's go brainstorm.'

There went her chin again. 'You're not just raising money—you have a hands-on plan that will help some of those homeless kids out there. That's pretty big in my book, and nothing you say will change my opinion. Now, we'd better find Tony and say goodbye.'

One effusive farewell later and they were outside. Next to him, Ruby inhaled the cold crisp air and looked up into the darkness of the sky. 'Do you think it will snow?'

'Unlikely.'

'So no white Christmas?' Ruby said with a hint of wistfulness. 'It's a shame, really—can you imagine how beautiful Cornwall would be covered in snow?' She shook her head. 'On the subject of Christmas…how do you feel about a Christmas party at Caversham? Not on Christmas Day, obviously, but maybe Christmas Eve drinks? Or eve of Christmas Eve drinks? For suppliers and locals. A lot of the staff we've taken on are local, so I think it would be a nice idea. Bank some goodwill…show the Caversham community ethos.'

Ethan considered—it was a good idea. But not in the run-up to Christmas.

'It doesn't fit with my plans.' More plans he didn't wish to share. 'Maybe we could think about it later? After New Year? Anyway, I know you said you had Christmas plans as well. So take some time off. From the twenty-first—that's not a problem.'

'Okay. Thanks.'

Enthusiasm was not prominent in her voice and Ethan swallowed the urge to ask her exactly what her plans were. Not his business—and not fair, as he didn't want to share his own.

The limo pulled up and he held the door open for Ruby to slide in, averted his eyes from the smooth length of her leg, hoped the tantalising cinnamon smell wouldn't whirl his head further. *Employee, employee, employee.*

As soon as the car started she leant forward; now her enthusiasm shone through the dim interior of the car.

'So—for the medieval banquet…I've already done loads of research and I've got some fab dishes we could use. What do you think about eels in a thick spicy purée, loach in a cold green sauce and a meat tile—which is chicken cooked in a spiced sauce of pounded crayfish tails, almonds and toasted bread, garnished with whole crayfish tails. Or capon pasties—or even eel and bream pasties. I've spoken to a medieval re-enactor and I reckon he'll know someone who will come along and cook us some samples. We could even put together a recipe book and sell it—raise some extra funds.'

'Excellent ideas. Though…what is loach?'

'It's a freshwater fish. Mind you, I'm not sure you can get it here.' A quick rummage in her evening bag netted a small notebook and pen. 'I'll check. What about an auction?' A sudden grin illuminated her face. 'Hey! You could talk to Tony. Auction off a cooking lesson with Antonio Pugliano. What do you think?'

His breath caught as his lungs suspended their function. One thought only was in his mind—Ruby was so beautiful, so animated, so unutterably gorgeous, and all he wanted was to tug her across the seat and kiss her.

CHAPTER SEVEN

RUBY BROKE OFF as all her ideas took flight from her brain in one perfect V-shaped swoop, evicted by an across-the-board sweep of desire. Ethan's pupils had darkened and the atmosphere in the limousine morphed. Words withered on her tongue she shifted towards him, propelled by instinct, pulled by his mesmerising eyes.

His features seemed ever so slightly softened by the shadows in the dim interior. Or maybe it was because now she had gained some insight. This man cared about so much more than profit and business domination. He hadn't let ambition consume him to the point where he forgot people in need. Forgot the Ethan and Ruby of a decade ago.

'Ethan...' she whispered.

Somehow they were right alongside each other, her leg pressed against the solid strength of his thigh, and she let out a small sigh. The closeness felt right, and she twisted her torso so she faced him, placed a hand over his heart, felt the steady beat increase tempo. Then his broad, capable hand cupped her jaw oh so gently, his thumb brushed her lip and she shivered in response.

His grey-blue eyes locked onto hers with a blaze of desire that melted all barriers, called to something deep inside her. She parted her lips, sheer anticipation hollowed her tummy—and then with precipitous speed his expression changed.

'What am I doing?'

The words were muttered with a low ferocity as his hand dropped from her face, left her skin bereft.

He hauled in an audible breath. 'This is not a good idea. I wish it were, but it isn't.'

It took a few seconds for the words to register, to make sense, and then reality hit. Forget Ethan. What was *she* doing? This was her boss…this was Ethan Caversham…this was a disastrous idea.

The idea that a reporter with some sort of lens able to penetrate tinted windows might have caught them on camera made her cringe. But even worse than that was the sheer stupidity of getting involved in any way with Ethan. There was an edge of danger—a foreshadow she recognised all too well and that urged her to scramble back to her side of the seat.

'You're right. I…I guess we got carried away. Food, champagne, limo… It's easily done. We'll forget it ever happened, yes? But would you mind if we took up the brainstorming tomorrow?'

She needed time to detonate that near-kiss from her psyche, scrub it from her memory banks. Right now the idea of Ethan in her suite was impossible to contemplate. A few hours by herself and she would rebuild the façade, resume the role of Ruby Hampton, Restaurant Manager. Then all would be well—because this time the mask would be uncrackable, fireproof, indestructible…

Unable to stop herself, she glanced nervously out of the window, checking for reporters.

Ethan noticed, and his lips pulled into a tight, grim line. 'Worried about the paps? You're safe in here, you know.'

'I know.'

And she did—deep down. Thanks to Ethan, who had neutralised the reporters with smooth, cold ease and rendered them powerless. The memory triggered a small thrill that she hastened to suppress. Yes, Ethan had protected her—but he had done so on principle. To him, the Hugh Farlanes and the paps out for a story at any price were scum and he would shield anyone from them. It wasn't personal. He would champion anyone broken or wounded or hurt.

But that near-kiss was pretty personal, pointed out a small inner voice. Which was exactly why he'd shut it down. And she should be grateful for that—would be once she'd escaped this limousine, where the air swirled with might-have-beens and what-ifs.

When they arrived back at the castle Ruby practically shot from the car through the grand entrance. 'I'll see you in the morning,' she called over her shoulder.

An expletive dropped from Ethan's lips, making her pause and turn on the stairs. He scrubbed a hand down his jaw, looking weary.

'Listen, Ruby, we need to get rid of the awkwardness. We have a lot to do in a minimal amount of time to upgrade the opening dinner to a ball. So we must manage it—nothing happened and nothing will happen. It was one fool moment and I will not let that ruin the professional relationship we have established.'

'You're right. It wasn't even a kiss. No big deal, right?'

An infinitesimal hesitation and then he nodded. 'No big deal.'

* * *

Ethan's head pounded as he looked across at Ruby. Seated at her desk she was back in professional mode—glossy black hair pinned back into a svelte chignon, dressed in dark grey trousers and a pinstripe jacket over a crisp white shirt. Her posture spoke of wariness and her eyes held a matching guard. The spontaneous trust, the spark doused and if Ethan could have worked out a way to kick himself round Cornwall he would have.

She straightened some papers on her desk, the action unnecessary. 'If it's OK with you rather than brainstorm I'll put together a presentation.'

Which meant he'd miss out on seeing her features light with enthusiasm as she came up with ideas. Mind you it was that illumination that had led to his disastrous impulse the night before. Impulses never ended well—he knew that to bitter cost.

Ruby was a woman with a plan to have a family—she was barely out of a demoralising relationship, and he had no business kissing her. 'Sounds good. Come down to my office when you're ready.' Maybe he'd rustle up some stilts to shore up the conversation. As he clicked the door shut he vowed to himself that by hook or by crook he'd win back their former camaraderie. It was necessary in order to maximise their productivity and their ability to pull of this ball. It was zip to do with a desire to see her lips curve up into a genuine smile.

So first he'd throw himself into work, get himself back on track and then he'd charm Ruby back to the status quo. But one conference call later a perfunctory knock heralded the appearance of Ruby and camaraderie looked to be the last thing on her mind—in fact she could have personified the cliché spitting mad.

'I have a message for you.' Annoyance clipped each syllable.

'Shoot.'

Her chest rose and he could almost see metaphorical steam issuing from her. 'It's from Tony Pugliano.'

Ah... 'Why didn't you put the call through to me?'

'Obviously I tried to, but you were engaged, and then Tony said it didn't matter—he could discuss it with me. Which was when he informed me that he will make a delivery of super-special pizzas on the twenty-second of December. Explained how happy he is to support such a worthy cause and how much he admires your plan to give these teens in care a wonderful time over the Christmas period. So there you go—message delivered.'

With that she swivelled on one black-booted foot and headed for the door.

That wasn't just anger that radiated off her—there was hurt as well.

'Ruby—wait.'

A heartbeat of hesitation and then she turned to face him. 'Yes.'

'I should have told you.'

Her shoulders lifted. 'It's your business—you don't have to tell me everything.'

'No. But I should have told you this.'

'So why didn't you?'

'We have been and will be working full-time until the ball. I figured you'd deserve a break—those days will be pretty full-on. Plus the kids will be here from the twenty-second to the twenty-fourth, and I know you have Christmas plans. I didn't want you to feel obliged to cancel them, or to feel guilty. It's no big deal.'

All the truth—though nowhere near the complete truth. But it was difficult to explain his utter disinclination to let her see the full extent of his charitable activities.

Her expression softened as she studied his face, though a small frown still nipped at her wide brow. 'Your idea of what is a big deal and mine is different. But you're right—you should have told me. Now I know, I would like to help.'

Bad idea… The previous night had amply demonstrated that a break would do them good. 'No need. I have it all covered here. There is nothing for you to do—so go and enjoy yourself.'

'Ethan, I don't want to go and enjoy myself. I know I can help. Why don't you want me to? Is it because…?' Her voice faltered for a second and then she met his gaze full-on. 'Because of what happened last night.'

'No. I don't want you to help because I don't want you to get burn out. There is a huge amount of work to be done in the next few days. You'll need a break. I've got it covered.'

Ethan could feel the grooves in the floor where his heels were dug in. Instinct told him that if they weren't careful, complications would abound.

'I bet you haven't.' Her chin angled, pugnacious. 'Tell me your plans and if I can work out how to improve them I get to help. Deal?'

Great! Instinct had made another express delivery—this was über-important to Ruby and it went deep, though he wasn't sure why.

Expelling a sigh of pure exasperation, he shrugged. 'Fine. I wanted to do it all actually on Christmas Day, but that didn't work out. So...a busload of teenagers will arrive here on the twenty-second. They are all either in children's homes or in foster care and they've all got a chequered history. We'll have a pizza, DVD and games night. I've ordered a billiards table and a darts board. On the twenty-third I and a few surf instructors will take them out for a day of water sports. We'll come back and I'm having caterers in to serve up a Christmas dinner. Another relaxed games evening, then to bed. Another morning's water sport on Christmas Eve and then they head back.'

There—you couldn't say fairer than that surely? So who knew why Ruby was shaking her head?

'What you have scheduled is brilliant, but I can make it better,' she said flatly.

'How?'

'Can I sit?'

Once he'd nodded she lowered herself onto a chair, rested her elbows on the desk and cupped her chin.

'I think you've missed something.'

'What? Another game? A...?'

'The magic of Christmas. You've mentioned Christmas dinner, but otherwise it could be any weekend. This is about the spirit of Christmas even if it's not actually Christmas Day. So what about a tree?'

'I thought about that and I figured the last thing they'll want is a tree and lots of schmaltz. These kids are tough and they've been through the mill. They'll want to obliterate Christmas—suppress the tainted memories it evokes.'

'Maybe some of them think like that—maybe that's what they need to think in order to get through Christmas. Dissing Christmas is their method of self-defence. But deep down they are still kids, and they deserve to be given a real Christmas—to see that Christmas doesn't always have to suck, that it can be wonderful and magical. It could be that what they're going back to is dismal, or lonely, or grim, so this two days you give them has to be something precious. Maybe to help them dilute those tainted memories.'

Her words strummed him... They spoke of a deep, vibrant sincerity and an underlying genuine comprehension, and Ethan knew that such empathy could only come from one place.

'Were you ever in care?' he asked. 'Is that why this is so important to you?'

She blinked, as if the question had zinged out of nowhere and caught her completely on the hop, skip and jump.

A flush seeped into her cheeks and then she shrugged. 'Yes—and yes. I was in care, and that's why I want to be part of this. I was eleven when it happened, and although I know that foster care can sometimes work out well it didn't for me. Looking back, I can see I was a difficult child to care for—so no surprise that I was moved from place to place. Including a stint in a residential home. I empathise with these kids. Because I remember vividly how awful holiday times were. Especially Christmas. But that doesn't mean I've given up on Christmas. And I don't want these kids to either.'

'I'm sorry the care system didn't work for you.'

'Don't be. I'm not after sympathy. I'm after your agreement to let me loose on this Christmas break. What do you think?'

Ethan drummed his fingers on the table. Of course he could shut this down and tell her no, but what kind of heel would that make him? To turn away someone who fervently wanted to help with a cause he fervently believed in?

'Go for it. You have carte blanche.' His smile twisted a little 'If you can give these kids some of the magic of Christmas then that would be a great thing. But I'm not sure it'll be easy. Some of these kids come from a very notorious estate and they have all been in serious trouble at one time or another.'

Images of the estate dotted his retina like flash photography. Depressing grey high-rise buildings, tower blocks of misery, with the smell of urine up the stairs, lifts that never worked. Vandalised park areas daubed with graffiti where kids roamed in gangs, so many of them caught in a vicious cycle of young offenders' units and truancy, the product of misery and neglect. Guilt stamped him—because he hadn't had that excuse for the road he'd chosen to walk.

Suddenly aware of Ruby's small frown, he shook his head to dislodge the thoughts. 'Just keep it in mind that you may need more than a magic wand and sprinkle of glitter,' he said.

'Sure...'

The speculative gaze she planted on him sent

a frisson of unease through him. It was as if she were considering waving that wand and glitter pot at him.

He tugged his keyboard across the desk. 'Now you're here let's start that brainstorm session and get down to business.'

Time to make it clear this was a non-magical, glitter-free zone.

CHAPTER EIGHT

'THROUGH HERE, PLEASE.'

Two days later Ruby directed the three men toting the most enormous Christmas tree she'd ever seen into the library—the room Ethan had designated as Teen Base.

'That's perfect,' she stated, refusing to allow the battalion of doubts that were making a spirited attempt to gain a foothold in her brain.

It was the tyrannosaurus rex of spruces. Once the delivery men had left she contemplated the sheer enormity of actually decorating the tree, and for a second considered enlisting Ethan's help.

No. The tree had been her idea—plus she had vowed not to orchestrate any time with Ethan that could be avoided. Somehow she had to squash the urge to try to entice him into the idea of liking Christmas—had to suppress the urge for closeness that threatened at every turn.

The problem was the more they discussed the medieval ball and ways to raise money and publicity for their cause, the more she learnt about his ideas for Caversham Castle and the worse her gooey tummy syndrome became. The more he spoke about the youths he wished to help, the more sure she was that his empathy came from his own experiences. Which in turn led to her nutty desire to enmesh Ethan in the magic of Christmas.

Only it was clear he had no wish to enter her net. In the past two days his demeanour had been always professional, with the high expectations she'd become accustomed to, alleviated by a polite charm and appreciation for her work. But there was a guardedness, a caginess that kept her at a distance.

A distance she needed to respect—to welcome, even. Because Ethan Caversham was synonymous with danger. It was an equation she had to remember—because linked to her desire for emotional intimacy was the ever-present underlay of attraction. It was a lose-lose situation all round.

So she'd better get on with the decorations herself.

Inhaling the evocative spruce aroma that now tinged the air, Ruby opened the first box of ornaments with a small sigh of pleasure. This tree would exude Christmas and be the Christmassiest tree ever seen. Or at least the bits she could reach would be...

'Ruby.'

The sound of Ethan's deep voice nearly sent her tumbling from the stepladder.

'Here you are. We're meant to be doing the final run-through of the seating plan.'

Ruby twisted round to face him. 'I am so sorry. I lost track of time.'

'No worries.' His glance rested for a second on the tree. 'Looks good.'

'Good? Is that all you can say.' Ruby stepped backwards to assess her handiwork so far. 'It's flipping marvellous, if I say so myself. I know I've only managed to get less than half done, but I think the bold and beautiful theme works.'

Reds, purples and golds abounded, though she had made sure that the lush green of the pine was also on display. The ornaments were tasteful, but with a vibrant appeal that she thought would at least mean the tree would be noticed.

'So come on. Surely you can do better than "good" as an adjective.'

'Eye-catching,' he said, and she frowned at the obvious effort.

The syllables sounded forced. It was almost as

if he didn't want to look at the tree or at her. Well, tough! He'd agreed to her plan to try to offer these youths some Christmas spirit, so the least he could do was be polite.

Better yet… 'Do you want to help me finish decorating it? As you can see it's pretty big—and you're taller than me. Plus it might be fun.'

The challenging smile slid from her lips as she clocked his sudden leaching of colour, his small step backwards. As if he'd seen a ghost.

He scraped a hand down his face as if to force his features into a semblance of normality. 'I'll pass, thanks. Trust me—you wouldn't want me bah-humbugging about the place.'

It was a credible attempt to lighten his expression, marred only by the wary ice-blue flecks in his eyes and the slight clenching of his jaw.

Every instinct told her he was hurting, and without thought she moved towards him and placed her hand over his forearm—the texture of his skin, the rough smattering of hair embedded itself into her fingertips.

'Look what happened to Scrooge. The ghosts of Christmases Past do not have to ruin the possibilities of Christmas Present.'

She'd expected him to scoff at the concept of

ghosts—instead he simply shook his head. There was something intangible about him that she didn't understand—the way his blue-grey eyes zoned in on her, haunted, glittering with something elusive, as if they could see something she couldn't.

'Leave it, Ruby. The tree is incredible; you're doing a great job. Find me when it's done. No rush.'

His voice was so flat that instinct told her his spectres hovered close. It seemed clear what she ought to do—let him go, remember his disinclination to get close, the danger signs she had already identified, his need for distance. But she couldn't… She didn't know what had triggered his reaction, doubted he would tell her, but maybe she could help.

'Don't go.'

A frown descended on his brow at her words and she clenched her fingers into her palm and forced herself to hold her ground.

'Ethan. Stay. Try it. Let's decorate together.'

Gathering all her courage, she squatted down and hefted a box of purple baubles.

'Here. I get that you don't want to, and I get that sometimes the past taints the present, but these kids will be here the day after tomorrow and there's lots to be done.'

'You're suggesting tree decoration as some form of therapy?' He was back in control now—on the surface at least—and his voice was a drawl. 'Or have you bitten off more than you can chew?'

'A bit of both… This tree needs help. So—are you in?'

Was he in? Ethan stared down at the box of purple ornaments. Why was he even considering this idea?

Because Ruby had a point. From a practical point of view this gargantuan tree did need to be finished, and if he left Ruby to it she probably wouldn't get it done until past midnight.

And that was a problem because…?

Ruby was the one who had ordered the tree in the first place—and since when had he cavilled at the thought of his staff working overtime? Ethan gusted out a sigh. Since now, apparently. Because—tough business guy or not—if he walked out of this room now he would feel like an A-class schmuck.

He'd have to get over the memories and get on with it.

The shock had hit him with unexpected force. For a vivid second the memory of Tanya had been so stark he might have believed he'd been transported back in time. He'd heard his sister's voice persuading him to help decorate the tree, remembered arranging the tinsel and the scruffy, cheap but cheerful decorations under her instruction.

The memory had receded now, and as he looked at Ruby's almost comically hopeful expression he shrugged.

'I'm in.'

That way maybe there'd be a chance of getting some actual work done that day.

Whoa, Ethan, play fair. He'd agreed to this whole magic of Christmas idea; he just hadn't reckoned on the extent of Ruby's enchantment scheme.

'Excellent,' she said. 'So you're in charge of purple. I'll do the red.'

For a while they worked in a silence that seemed oddly peaceful. To his own irritation he found himself stepping down at intervals, to check the effect of his handiwork. A snort of exasperation escaped his lips and Ruby's subsequent chuckle had him glaring across at her.

'Sorry. I couldn't help it. You look so...*absorbed*.'

'Yes, well. If I do something I make sure I do it properly.'

For no reason whatsoever the words travelled across the pine-scented air and took on an unintended undertone...one that brought an image of kissing Ruby with attention to every detail. It was an effort not to crane his neck in a search for mistletoe. Instead his eyes snagged on the lush outline of her lips and desire tautened inside him.

Her fingers rose and touched her lips. He heard her intake of breath and forced his gaze to return to the tree.

'So...' His voice resembled that of a frog. *Try again*. 'So, believe me, my share of this tree will rock and roll.'

A small shake of her head and then her lips tilted into a full-wattage smile. 'See? It is kind of fun, isn't it?'

Ethan blinked—to his own surprise, it was... but it would be a whole lot better if he could tell himself that the reason had zip to do with his fellow decorator. Maybe her palpable belief in the magic of Christmas was contagious. Dear Lord— he'd lost the plot big-time. If he didn't take care he'd find himself with a pillow round his middle in a red suit.

'Could be worse,' he muttered as he stretched up his arm to thread a silver-spangled ball on to a branch.

Hmm... Alarm bells started to toll in his brain. If Ruby had gone this over the top with the tree, what other schemes were afoot?

'So...any other magical plans apart from the tree?'

Ruby expertly unhooked a strand of tinsel and rearranged it. 'I've planned a bake-off.'

'A bake-off?'

'Yup. I think they'll go for it because of all the TV shows. My plan is that everyone has a go at Christmas cookies and gingerbread. It will be friendly—they can judge each other. Or the ones who really don't want to bake can judge. It will make a nice start to the festivities. Then they can eat Tony's pizzas and chill, play some games, maybe catch a Christmas movie. I'll make pop-corn.'

'That sounds like a lot of work for you.' Ethan hesitated; he didn't want to hail on her parade or dim her enthusiasm, but... 'You do know that these kids…they may not appreciate your good intentions.'

'Don't worry. I know I'm coming across all Pollyanna, but I have kept a reality check. I've got in extra fire extinguishers, plus I've cleared out all the sharp knives, though I've decided cookie cutters won't be lethal. I know there is a chance none of them will engage. But…' Reaching up, she attached a gold bauble. 'I've got to try. Because if we get through to even one of these kids and create a happy memory of Christmas then it will be worth it. Even if they aren't in a place to show their appreciation.'

'The "dilute the tainted memories" approach?' he said.

'Yup.'

For a second Ethan wondered if that were possible—then knew he was deluded. It wasn't. He wasn't even sure he wanted it to be.

Once he'd believed the best thing to do was obliterate the chain of memories with mindless anger. Beat them into oblivion. Especially the memory of the Christmas after Tanya's death. His mother, him, and the ghost of Tanya. In the end rage had overcome him and he'd hurled the microwaved stodgy food at the wall, watched the gravy trickle and blend in with the grungy paint. Once he'd started he hadn't been able to stop—had pulled the scrawny tree from its pot, flung it down. Stamped on it, kicked it—as if the tree had been the bully who had driven Tanya to her death.

His mother hadn't said a word; then she had left the room with a curt, 'Clean it up.'

Seconds later he'd heard the sound of the television and known that it was the end of Christmas. By the following Christmas she'd consigned him to social services and he'd taken to the streets, consumed by grief, anger and misery. Then finally he'd decided to take control—to leash the demons and channel his emotions in order to succeed.

With an abrupt movement he stood back. 'I'm done.'

Seeing the snap of concern in her blue eyes, he forced his lips into a smile. Ruby's way wasn't his way, but that wasn't to say it wasn't a good way—and she was right. If her way could help even one of these teenagers then it was worth every moment.

'It looks spectacular.'

That pulled an answering smile, though her

eyes still surveyed him with a question. 'It's a work of art.'

It was definitely a work of *something*—though Ethan wasn't sure what.

'Hang on,' she said. 'We need to do the star. It's the *pièce de résistance*.' She walked across the room and rummaged around in a box before twirling round. 'What do you think?'

Ethan blinked, all darkness chased away by a star that could only be described as the Star of Bling. 'Wow. That's…'

'Eye-catching?' Ruby handed it up to him. 'I think you should do the honours. Really.' Her voice softened. 'This is your scheme. I know I'm banging on about the magic of Christmas, but without you these teens wouldn't be going any-where. So I think it's right that you should put the star on top.'

Ethan hesitated, a frisson of discomfort rippling through him at her tone. Too much admiration, too much emotion…best to get this whole inter-lude over with.

In an abrupt movement he placed the star on top of the tree, nestled it into the branches and jumped down off the stepladder.

'There. Done. Now, how about we get some work done?'

'Sure…'

Ethan frowned at the note of hesitation in her voice, saw her swift glance at her watch and sighed. 'Unless you have more Christmas magic to sort?'

'Not magic…just something I need to do. But I can do it later. It's not a problem.'

Curiosity warred with common sense and won. 'Okay. I'll bite. What needs to be done?'

'Now I'll sound like Pollyanna on a sugar rush. I've bought them all gifts. Out of my own money,' she added quickly.

'The money's not an issue.' Affront touched him that she'd thought it would be.

'I know that! I just wanted to make it personal. I'll sign the tags from you as well. Though it would be better if you—' She broke off.

'If I signed them myself? I can do that.'

'Fabulous. I'll run up and get all the gifts now. Maybe we could wrap them whilst we discuss the seating plan?'

Ethan opened his mouth and then closed it again. What he'd meant was that Ruby could give him the tags to sign. No need for him to see the pres-

ents—presumably she'd bought them all chocolates or key rings. But she looked so pleased…

'Sure,' he heard his voice say.

'I'll be back in a mo…'

'Bring them to my office.' At least that way he
could pretend it was work.

Ruby toted the bags out of her bedroom and
paused on the landing. Time for a pep talk. It was
wonderful that Ethan had bought into her ideas,
but she had to grab on to the coat-tails of perspective before it disappeared over the horizon.
Sure, he'd helped decorate the tree, but that was
because she had given him little choice—he'd
done it for those teens and so that she could resume her restaurant manager duties more quickly.
Not for *her*.

It was time to get these gifts wrapped and get
on with some work.

So why, when she entered his office, did she
feel a small ripple of disappointment to see Ethan
behind his desk, intent on his computer screen,
exuding professionalism?

His glance up as she entered was perfunctory
at best.

She hesitated. 'If you want to get on with some
work I can wrap these later.'

'No, it's fine.' One broad hand swept the contents of the desktop to one side.

'Right. Here goes. I've got a list that details each person and their gift.'

His body stilled. 'You bought individual gifts?'

'Yes. I called the social workers, got a few numbers for foster carers and residential home workers and chatted to some people. Just to find out a bit about them all, so I could buy something personal.'

His eyes rested on her with an indecipherable expression.

'Hey… Like you would say, it's no big deal.'

'Yes, it is.'

'No—really. To be honest, it's kind of therapeutic. In a weird way I feel like I'm doing it for myself. The me of all those years ago. Because I can remember what it was like in care, being the person with the token present. That was the worst of it—having to be grateful for gifts that were impersonal. Don't get me wrong—some carers really tried. But they didn't know me well enough to know what I wanted. Others couldn't be bothered to get to know me. So I'd get orange-flavoured chocolate when I only liked milk, or a top that I loathed and that didn't fit.'

For heaven's sake!

'That all sounds petty, doesn't it? But I want these kids to get a gift they *want*—not something generic.'

'Like a key ring or a chocolate bar?' he said, and a rueful smile touched his lips.

'Is that what you thought I'd bought?'

'Yes. I guess I should have known better.' Ethan rose to his feet. 'Come on.'

'Where to?'

'Let's do this properly. We'll wrap in the bar and you can show me what you bought everyone and brief me on what you found out about them. I'll light the fire and we'll have a drink.'

'What about work?'

The rueful smile became even more rueful, mixed with charm, and Ruby concentrated on keeping her breathing steady.

'I think we have done all we can do. The seating plan looks fine, the food is sorted, the wine is sorted, the auction is sorted and the band is booked. The banqueting hall furniture arrives after the Christmas period. All in all, I think we may have run out of work.'

He was right—and she knew exactly why that smile was now packed with regret...because without work to focus on what would they do with themselves?

She looked down at the presents she carried. The answer to that problem was to wrap fast, then flee to bed. *Alone.*

CHAPTER NINE

Ruby watched as Ethan lit the fire, his movements deft, the tug of denim against the muscles of his thighs holding her gaze as he squatted by the flames.

Stop with the ogling.

She forced herself to lay out the silver paper patterned with snowflakes and the list of gifts on the table. A sip of the deep red wine Ethan had poured for them both and then she waited until he sat opposite her.

'Here,' she said, and handed over the first present. 'This one is for Max: he's one of the boys in residential care and he's really into music—specifically rap, which I have to admit I know nothing about. So I did some research, conferred with his key worker at the home, and we came up with this T-shirt. It's the right size, and it's a cool label, so...'

Ethan shook the T-shirt out and nodded approval at the slogan. Folding it up again, he kept his eyes on her. 'It must have taken a fair amount of time to research each and every one of them and then find what you wanted. You should have told me. I'd have lightened your workload.'

'No way. I was happy to do it on my own time. Plus, you've hardly been idle yourself. You've briefed the surf instructors, sourced the caterers, the billiards table, co-ordinated all the paperwork—and you're also running a global business.'

Ruby frowned, wondering why he never seemed to realise just how much he did.

He broke off a piece of tape with a deft snap. 'What I've done is generic—I could have set this up for any group of teenagers in care. You've made it personal.'

'Yes, I have. But I couldn't have done that if you hadn't set it up in the first place. Plus…' She hesitated. 'What you've done is personal too. You're giving them what helped you. The opportunity to surf, to do other water sport, to expend energy and vent frustration in a positive way. So what you've done isn't generic, and I won't let you believe it is. You care about these kids.' With a sudden flash of insight she blurted, 'Did *you* grow up on an estate? Like the one some of these kids are from?' The one he'd described as 'notorious'.

For a second she thought he wouldn't answer; the only sound was the crackle of the logs. Then he dropped the wrapped T-shirt into a bag and lifted his broad shoulders in an I-suppose-there's-no-harm-in-answering shrug.

'Yes, I did. So I relate to where these kids have come from—a tough background, maybe abuse, neglect, parents on drugs and alcohol or in prison. It's easy for them to get into trouble, join a gang, because there's nothing else to do and no one to stop them. And then they do what their parents did—steal, deal…whatever it takes. All these kids are in that cycle, and I'd like to show them there are other choices. Not just by giving them Christmas, but by giving them incentive. If they can go away from here and stay clean for a few months they can come back and take other opportunities if they want to. I want to give them a chance to get off the wheel.'

'Like you did?'

'No.'

His voice was harsh now, and the dark pain that etched his features made her yearn to reach out.

'I didn't have their excuse. My dad was a low-life—apparently he yo-yoed in and out of prison—but my mum tossed him out when I was tiny.

The time he went down for armed robbery she said enough was enough. Mum didn't drink or do drugs, and any neglect was because she was out at work all day so she could put food on the table. God knows, she did her best—but it wasn't enough. I jumped onto the wheel all by myself. Like father, like son.'

The words sounded like a quote, the derision in them painful, and Ruby tried to gather her scrambled thoughts. 'I'm guessing you got into trouble—but it's like you said yourself. In an environment like a troubled estate that's understandable. The point is you got off that wheel and out of trouble. Look at you now—your mum must be proud.'

It was the wrong thing to have said; his face was padlocked and his eyes flecked with ice. Surely his mother hadn't been the one to make the father-son comparison?

Disbelief morphed into anger as she saw his expression. 'You are *not* a lowlife.'

'That's a matter of opinion.' His eyes were dark now, his voice vibrating with mockery, though she wasn't sure if he was mocking her, himself or the world.

'I don't care. Opinion doesn't make you into

your father. It doesn't work like that. I know that because *I* am not my parents. Not either of them. And I never will be.'

Her fingers clenched around the edges of the table as she faced him.

'My parents were addicts. Booze, heroin—whatever they could get their hands on, whenever they could get their hands on it. At whatever cost. Food and paying bills and shoes were all irrelevant.'

She gestured down to the reams of Christmas wrapping paper.

'For them the festive period was an excuse to justify extra excess—which led to extra verbal violence or extra apathy. Turkey, decorations and presents didn't feature.'

For a moment she was back there—in the past. Feeling the tingle of childish anticipation that scratched her eyelids as she lay on the verge of sleep. The twist of hope that Santa was real…that she'd open her eyes and see four stuffed stockings for her siblings and herself. More importantly her parents, groomed and sober, would watch them opening them with love. Then reality would touch her with the cold fingers of dawn. The smell of stale cigarettes and worse would invade her nostrils and she'd know it would be another Christmas of playing avoid-the-abuse and hide-from-notice, ensuring her siblings stayed out of the line of fire.

The memory gave steel to her voice. 'I am not like them. I won't ever let addiction become more important than my children. *Ever.*'

His hands clenched on his thighs and his whole body vibrated with tension. His foot jumped on the wooden floor. As if he wanted to somehow change her past for her.

'Ruby. I am so sorry. I don't know what to say—except that it sucks that you had to go through that.'

She gave an impatient shake of her head. 'It did suck, but that's not the point. The point is *I* am not my parents and *you* are not your father.' His jaw was set and she could almost see her statement slide off him unheeded. 'I mean, do you even know where he is now?'

'No. My guess would be in a prison cell.'

'Well, you aren't. You are here, trying to make a difference and do good.'

'In which case I'd better get on with it.' His tone was light, but with an edge that emphasised the end of the subject. 'But first...' and now his gaze was filled with warmth and compassion '...I can't imagine what you went through, but I am full of admiration for the wonderful woman that child has become.'

'Thank you.'

Frustration mixed with a yen to get close to him—to make him see that his achievements deserved kudos just as much as hers. Yet already she could see the shutters had been pulled down to hood his eyes as he picked up the tape again.

'We'd better get a move on,' he said. It's a big day tomorrow.'

'Wait.'

Something—she had to do *something*. Loathing touched her soul at the idea that Ethan had such a deep-rooted, downright skewed vision of himself. Without allowing herself time to think she moved round the table and took his hand, tugged at it to indicate she wanted him to stand. He rose to his feet and she kept her fingers wrapped around his, tried to ignore the frisson that vibrated through her at the feel of his skin against hers.

'Come here.'

The small frown deepened on his forehead as she led him to the ornate gold Victorian mirror— an oval of gilt curls and swirls.

'Look at yourself,' she said firmly, 'and you will see you. Ethan Caversham. You are you. You may look like your dad, but you are not like him. This I know.'

His reluctance palpable, he shrugged. But he complied, and as he glanced at his reflection she hoped against all hope that he would see what she could. It was an optimism that proved fool-hardy as his jaw hardened and a haunting mock-ery speckled his blue-grey eyes.

She stepped forward and turned so that she faced him, stood on tiptoe and cupped his jaw in her palms. The six o'clock shadow was rough against her skin as she angled his face and met his gaze.

'You are a good man,' she whispered, and reached up to kiss him.

Heaven knew she'd had every intention of pressing her lips to his cheek, but instinct over-came common sense and the burning of need to imprint her sincerity onto his consciousness pre-vailed. Her lips brushed his and she gave a small sigh as desire shimmered and sizzled, and then his broad hands spanned her waist and pulled her against him.

For a second she thought he'd kiss her properly, deepen the connection that fizzed, but as if he'd suddenly caught sight of his reflection he gently moved her away and stepped backwards instead. He lifted a hand and ran a finger against her cheek in a gesture so gentle she felt tears threaten.

'Thank you, Ruby. I appreciate the endorsement.'

A smile redolent with strain touched his lips and then he turned and headed back to the table, sat down and picked up the scissors.

This was a *good* thing, right? Of course it was. Kissing Ethan was a bad, bad idea—that was an already established fact. So she needed to crush the absurd sense of disappointment and follow suit.

Two days later Ethan watched the busload of teenagers depart round the curve of the driveway. A sideways glance showed Ruby still waving, a smile on her face, though he knew she must be exhausted.

'Come on,' he said. 'I'll make you a cheese toastie and a cup of tea.'

'We've just had lunch.'

'No. You just made everybody else lunch. You didn't actually eat. No protests.'

'Okay. I am hungry. Thank you.'

Twenty minutes later he made his way to the

lounge, to find her curled up on an overstuffed armchair, dark head bent over her phone as she texted.

'Hey...' she said, looking up as he deposited the tray on a small table next to her. 'I'm texting Tara. To tell her I meant it when I said I'd keep in touch.'

Her expression was serious, her brow creased, as she picked up the sandwich.

He eased onto the sofa opposite and stretched his legs out. 'You bonded with her, didn't you?'

'Hard *not* to bond with someone who scares the bejesus out of you!'

Ethan shook his head; he could still feel the cold glug of panic that had hit his gut two days earlier.

Everything had been going so well. Nearly all the kids had wanted to have a go at the bake off, and had gathered in the kitchen with no more than some minor banter. Ruby had set up each person with a station with all the ingredients set out. There were recipes and she was at the front to demonstrate the technique. There had been a few flour-bomb incidents but after a couple of interventions by the social worker they settled down and soon everyone had been absorbed in the tasks at hand. The scent of cinnamon and gin-

ger pervaded the kitchen and Ethan had relaxed enough to start a conversation about the following day's surf trip.

It had all happened so fast.

A dark-haired boy had been in discussion with his neighbour a blonde petite teenager. Ethan clocked the violent shake of her head and just as his antennae alerted him that there was trouble, the youth stepped too close. Uttered a profanity so crude Ruby's head whipped round from where she'd been helping someone else. As Ethan headed over, the girl whipped out a flick knife.

Ethan's lips straightened to grim as he strode forward but before he could get there Ruby had put herself directly in the girl's path and Ethan's gut froze. The girl looked feral, her pupils wide and he could only hope that she wasn't doped up on anything.

The knife glinted in her hand. Behind Ruby, the dark-haired boy had tensed and Ethan knew any second now the situation would blow. No way would that boy be able to keep face if he backed down to a girl—the only reason he hadn't launched yet was the fact that Ruby was in the middle.

She held her hand out to the girl. 'Tara, give me

the knife. No one is going to hurt you. Not now and not later. Not Max, not anyone.' Ruby's voice betrayed not a flicker of fear. She swept a glance at Ethan and gave a small shake of head and he slowed his stride. Ruby clearly didn't want him to spook the girl. Instead Ethan ducked round so that he could manoeuvre Max out of the equation, saw the boy open his mouth and moved straight in.

'Quiet.' Max took one look and kept his mouth shut.

'Come on, Tara,' Ruby said. 'It's OK. Look round. You're safe. Look at me. You have my word. Now give me the knife and it will all be fine.'

Tara had shaken her head. 'It'll never be fine,' she stated with a flat despair that chilled Ethan's blood. Then the knife fell to the floor, the clatter as it hit the tiles released some of the tension in the room. Ruby put her foot over the weapon, then stooped to pick it up.

'You want to keep going?' she asked Tara. 'It's OK. No repercussions.' She turned to Max and there was something in her stance that meant business. 'No repercussions,' she repeated.

Next to him Ethan saw the social worker open his mouth as if to intervene and he stepped into action. 'I second that. No repercussions from any-

one. This is not what this all about. You guys want to make a difference to your lives. It starts here. And this incident ends here.'

'Now back to baking,' Ruby said.

Looking back now, it occurred to Ethan how seamlessly he and Ruby had acted together, so attuned to the nuances of the scene, the risks, the threat, the best way to defuse the tension.

Ruby picked up her mug and cradled it. 'You know what she told me?'

Ethan shook his head. His chest panged at the pain sketched on Ruby's features.

'She told me she wished there *had* been repercussions. That if she'd ended up inside it would have been better for her than her life now.'

Ruby's voice was sad and heavy with knowledge.

'I don't blame her for having that knife. Her home life makes mine look like a picnic in the park. Her dad is a violent loser and she is so damaged no carer can cope. That's why she's in a residential home. That's why she reacted to Max like that—he was in her space and she panicked. Oddly enough after the incident Max tried to befriend her.' She glanced at him. 'Your doing?'

'I did talk to him.' He had tried to tell him there

were other ways—told him that there were consequences to actions.

'That's fab, Ethan. Maybe they can help each
other. I hope they'll all come back in September.
Once they let their guard down they were all so
full of potential—I mean, did you see them after
surfing? They had a blast.'

So had he. All the teenagers had been stoked
to be in the water and he'd watched them—some
of them carbon copies of himself and Rafael.
Tough...so tough...and always out to prove it.
Because if they didn't there was the fear of being
taken down. All swagger, all bravado—but up
against the waves, up against the spray and the
sea salt, they had met an element stronger than
themselves that they could challenge with impunity. And they'd loved it. Enough, he hoped, to
incentivise them to keep out of trouble until September.

A soft sigh escaped her lips. 'I wish...I wish I
could help. Take them all in and house the lot of
them.' She placed her empty plate down with a
thunk. 'Maybe one day I will. No—not maybe.
Definitely.'

'How are you going to do that?'

Her chin tilted. 'I'm going to adopt,' she said. 'That's my single parenthood plan.'

Maybe it shouldn't surprise him—after all, Ruby had been in care and he understood why she would want to help children like the child she had been. Hey, *he* wanted to do that. But adoption by herself...

Her eyes narrowed. 'You don't think it's a good plan?'

'I didn't say that.'

'Then what? You think I can't hack it?'

'I didn't say that either.'

'Then say something. What do you think?'

'I think it's a very, very big thing to take on.' He raised a hand. 'I'm not saying you couldn't do it. I think you would be a fantastic person for any kid to have in their lives.' And he meant that—he'd seen the way she'd interacted with all the kids, seen her capacity for care and love. 'But taking on older children... It's a huge commitment—especially on your own.'

'I know that.'

There was no uncertainty in her voice and he couldn't help but wonder at the depth of her need to do this even as he admired her confidence in herself. The idea of anybody—let alone a child...

let alone a child who had already been through the system—being dependent on him for their well-being made his veins freeze over. To those kids Ruby would be their salvation, and he knew that saving wasn't part of his make-up.

But concern still niggled. 'You said you'd decided on single parenthood because you can't pick good father material. Don't you think you should rethink that strategy?'

'What do you mean?'

'I mean why not open yourself up to the idea of a relationship? Find a man who will support you emotionally and be a great father to your family. You're too young to give up on having love and a family.'

'You have,' she pointed out.

'That's because I don't want love *or* a family. You can't give up on something you've never wanted in the first place. You do want love— you'd never have been sucked in by Hugh or those other two losers otherwise.'

'See?' Tucking her legs beneath her, she jabbed her finger at him. 'That's exactly it. Three out of three losers. That's a one hundred per cent miss rate. I can't risk what is most important to me— having a family—by taking a side quest for love.

Plus, if I pick wrong it could have a terrible effect on any children. I need to stay focused on my ultimate goal. I thought you of all people would get that. You want Caversham world domination and I want children. I won't be sidelined by anything else.'

Well, what could he say to that?

'I can see the "but" written all over your face, Ethan. I know it will be tough but it will be incredibly worthwhile.' The finality in her tone suggested that any argument would be futile. 'Like these past two days have been.'

'Two days is one thing. A lifetime is another.'

He pressed his lips together. Ruby was right—she had her goal and he had his, and hers was none of his business. What did he know? It was not as if he thought love was a good idea, so why push Ruby towards it? He didn't want the bright light of hope to be extinguished from those eyes by some idiot. But that wasn't his problem or his decision to make—it was Ruby's. So...

'You're right I think the past two days were a success—and a lot of that is thanks to you. The tree, the gifts, the food...and the karaoke carols were superb. You did a great job.'

Relief touched her face at the change of subject

and he wondered if she regretted telling him of her plans.

'So did you. Thanks muchly. And thanks for letting me be part of it.' A glance at her watch and she straightened up in the chair. 'Right. I'll start the clear-up procedure and then I'll be on my way. Leave you to your Christmas plans.'

Her voice was a smidge too breezy, and her eyes flicked away from his as she rose to her feet.

'Don't worry about clearing up,' he said as he stood, his eyes fixed on her expression. 'You've already spent so much time and effort on this—I want you to start your break as soon as possible.'

Deliberately casual, he stepped towards her.

'Where did you say you were going, again?'

'Um...' For a heartbeat she twisted her finger into a stray curl, then met his gaze with cool aplomb. 'I didn't.' As she moved towards the door she gave him a small smile. 'Any more than you shared *your* plans.'

Her pace increased to escape speed and instantly he moved to bar her path.

'That's easily remedied. My plan is to stay here.'

Surprise skittered across her face. 'Alone?'

'Yup. My original plan was to host the teens over Christmas—when that changed I didn't bother making different plans for Christmas Day. It's just another day, after all. But I know you don't agree with that. So what are your plans, Ruby?'

Her eyes narrowed slightly as she realised she'd walked straight into that. 'I... Look, why does it matter to you?'

'Because you have worked so hard, and made such a difference to those teenagers—I don't want to think that doing that has ruined your plans.'

'Oh. It hasn't. Truly.' A gust escaped her lips as he raised his eyebrows. 'You aren't going to let up, are you? Look, I haven't got any specific plans. I never did.'

A slight look of surprise tilted her features.

'It's odd, actually. My original plan was to shut myself away with some weepie movies and a vat of ice cream. But now I don't want to do that. In fact if I wanted to I could go out and paint the town red. Since your press release lots of people who had dropped me like the proverbial hot root vegetable are now keen to be my friend again. Or I could probably even rustle up an invite from a real friend. But I don't really want to do any of that either. So I think I'll just head home and use the time to relax. Read a book. Watch some sappy Christmas movies.'

Ever so slowly she started to edge around him for the door.

'Not so fast.' The idea flashed into his mind like a lightning bolt, zigzagged around and sparked a mad impulse. 'I have a better idea.'

'What?'

'Let's go away for Christmas.'

'Who? You and me?' Incredulity widened her eyes—clearly the idea was risible.

'Yup. We've worked incredibly hard and we deserve a break. You said you wanted snow—how about the Alps?'

The realisation that he was making this up as he went along triggered a ring tone of alarm.

'Are you serious?'

For a second excitement lit her blue eyes and Ethan ignored the warning blare of instinct—the reminder that mad impulses never ended well.

'Of course I'm serious. Why wouldn't I be?'

'Because… Well… We can't just up and leave.'

'Last time I looked I was the boss and I say we can.'

The idea gave him a sudden surge of exhilaration—the kind he usually felt on a surfboard. It morphed into a mad desire to take her hands and twirl her round the room. Which was every kind of nutty—from peanuts to Brazil. *Rein it in, Ethan.* What exactly was he suggesting, here?

Welcome rationalisation kicked in. 'I'd like to check out the Alps anyway—as a possible Caversham location.'

'But you haven't even opened the castle yet.'

Ethan shrugged. 'Gotta keep on moving, Ruby. I told you I want to make it big, and momentum is key.'

Plus, it made sense—it would make this a business trip and not a mad impulse at all. With any luck he'd get there, feel the buzz of a new venture—and the odd, unwanted emotions that Ruby stirred within him would dissipate. Come to that, once the ball was over—which was a few scant days away—he wouldn't need to spend as much time here. He'd see Ruby less, and his life would regain its status quo.

'So what do you think? Shall we go and get a feel for the place?'

Ruby wasn't sure she *could* think. Or at least think straight. His idea had conjured up cosy warm scenes. Snow, mountain peaks, magical Christmas card scenery... Ethan and Ruby walking hand in hand...

As if.

Ruby hauled in a breath and instructed her brain to think, to oust the temptation that had slunk to the table—a late and uninvited guest at negotiations. Ethan had probably never held hands with anyone in his life, and the very fact that the picture had formed in her mind meant she needed to be on her guard.

In fact… 'It's a crazy idea.'

'Why? We both deserve a break. I have a good gut feeling about the Alps as a Caversham location, you've done a lot of research into the Caversham ethos, and I'd value a second opinion from you.'

It all sounded so reasonable. His words slipped into her consciousness like honey. From a professional viewpoint her boss had asked her to go on a business trip. It was a no-brainer.

Plus, if she said no would he take someone else? A sudden vision of gorgeous blondes and curvy brunettes paraded in her brain and her nails scored into her palm in instinctive recoil.

'I think it sounds fabulous. Let's do it.'

Temptation gave a smug smile of victory and panic assailed her nerves. Because all of a sudden thrills of anticipation shot through her veins. *Chill, Ruby.* Who wouldn't look forward to Christmas in the Alps? Obviously those little pulse-buzzes had zilch to do with the prospect of one-on-one time with Ethan. Because that would be personal. To say nothing of certifiably stupid.

Ethan nodded, his expression inscrutable. 'Okay. I'll check flights and we'll take the first available one.'

'Fantastic.'

Though it occurred to Ruby that this whole idea could be better filed under 'Terminally Stupid'.

CHAPTER TEN

RUBY GLANCED ACROSS at Ethan and tried to stop her tummy from a launch into cartwheels. Tried to tell herself that her stomach's antics were a Braxton-Hicks-type reaction to non-existent air turbulence. Why on earth had she consented to this? Why in this universe had *he* suggested it?

Because it was work. That was why. Ethan wanted to scout out the French Alps and had decided that this was an ideal time. Plus he was a generous man, and this was his way of showing appreciation for all her hard work.

Work, Ruby. That was what this was and she had best remember that. After all it was Christmas Day, and apart from a perfunctory 'Merry Christmas' Ethan hadn't so much as referred to the fact.

Though she could hardly blame him. Organising their departure had been his priority, and she could only admire the efficiency that had achieved a super-early trip to her London apartment to pick up her passport, followed by a trip to the airport that had given her sufficient time to pick up the extra cold-weather clothes she needed as well as time for a spirited argument over who would pay for said clothing.

Now here they were, on board a flight to Geneva, where they would pick up a car. So who could blame Ethan for not making a hue and cry about it being Christmas—he was taking her to a magical Christmas place after all.

On a business trip.

What else did she want it to be?

Yet as she studied the strength of his profile, the potent force of his jaw, an obscure yearning banded her chest—as if she were a girl with her nose pressed against the glass pane of a sweet shop. Gazing, *coveting*, but unable to touch.

As if he sensed her gaze he turned to look at her and the breath hitched in her throat. The man was so gorgeous—but it was more than that. The way he had been with those teenagers had filled her with admiration. He'd shown them respect and invited respect in return—the fact that he'd cared about them had shone through, and it had triggered this ridiculous gooeyness inside her.

Enough. Say something. Before you embarrass yourself.

To her relief panic mobilised her vocal cords and she burst into speech. 'I was wondering—where are we staying?'

'The travel agent managed to find us a chalet; there weren't many options but she assured me that it would be perfect. And I've organised an itinerary.'

For a second his voice sounded almost gruff... even vulnerable...and she thought there was a hint of colour on the strong angles of his face.

'What sort of an itinerary?'

'The kind that will give us an idea of what other resorts offer.' Now his tone had segued to brusque—she was an idiot. What had she thought? That he'd picked things out for her?

'Great.'

The chalet was presumably part of a resort— which would be good. There would be hustle and bustle and other people, and they would be kept so busy with work that the two days would pass by in a flash.

'Sure is.' Ethan nodded a touch too enthusi- astically. 'I've got the address, so once we land we'll pick up the hire car, put the location into the satnav and be on our way.'

This had to be a joke right? Ethan stared through the windscreen of the four-by-four that had negotiated the curving mountain roads and treacherous hairpin bends to bring them to the chalet that the satnav had announced was their destination. He'd swear the robotic voice had a gloat to it.

He was going to track down that travel agent and have serious words. She had described the chalet as 'just the place' and left Ethan with the impression that it was part of a busy resort, awash with people and activities. Though maybe he'd been so distracted by Ruby, so caught up in the mad impulse of the moment, that he'd heard what he'd wanted to hear.

Because it turned out that the chalet was a higgledy-piggledy structure nestled in the fold of a valley and it looked like it had come straight out of a fairy tale. Set in a circular grove of snow-heaped birches, the property was made completely of wood. It practically *glowed*. Quaint wooden shutters boxed in the windows and there wasn't another person in sight.

It looked as if it had descended from the clouds especially for Christmas. It was a surprise that it wasn't wrapped up in festive paper with a bow on top.

Ethan resisted the urge to thunk his forehead on the chunky steering wheel. Instead he glanced across at Ruby, who had fallen asleep on the motorway and slept like the proverbial infant for the entire drive. Perhaps if he started the car he could drive them to the nearest hotel and blag them two rooms. Or he could phone the travel agent and...

Too late.

Next to him Ruby stretched sleepily and opened her eyes; her sleep-creased face looked adorably kissable.

'Can't believe I fell asleep.' Her blue eyes widened as she took in the scene. 'Oh, my goodness me! We get to stay here?'

'Looks like it.'

'It's as if we've been beamed into a fairy tale. Or a Christmas card.'

Or a nightmare.

'It's magical. I reckon it may even be made of gingerbread.'

'Which wouldn't exactly be very useful, would it?'

Chill, Ethan. Snapping wouldn't change the setting.

'Plus, I don't much want to be trapped in a cage by a wicked witch and fattened up. In fact maybe we should go and find somewhere else to stay.'

Her gurgle of laughter indicated that she'd missed the fact he'd meant it as a genuine suggestion. 'I didn't have you down as a fairy tale expert.'

'I'm not.'

For a second he remembered Tanya reading to him, his laughter at the funny voices she'd used for the different characters.

'You should go on stage,' he'd told her, and she'd shaken her head.

'I'd be too shy, Thanny,' she'd said in her soft voice. 'But I love reading to you.'

He pushed the memory away and glared at the chalet. 'I'm serious. Wouldn't you rather stay somewhere busier? Less isolated? Less over-the-top?'

'I…' She gave her head a small shake. 'Sorry, Ethan, I must still be half asleep. It just looks perfect for Christmas, but I guess it's not a good idea to stay somewhere so…' She trailed off.

So romantic, so small, so intimate.

Conversely the words challenged him—was he really saying that he was incapable of being in a romantic fairy tale chalet with Ruby? Talk about an overreaction. In truth the cutesy atmosphere should serve as a reminder that romance was anathema to him. Plus he could see from her expression that she had fallen for the place.

After the amount of work she'd put in these past weeks she deserved the chance to stay where she wanted to. With all she had been through in life she deserved a Christmas with some magic in it just as much as those teenagers had. Ethan might not believe in the magic of Christmas but Ruby Hampton did, and he would be a real-life Grinch if he denied her this.

'Why don't we go in and have a look round? Then decide what to do. The agent said the key would be outside, under a pot.'

Minutes later they crossed the threshold and irritation touched his brow as he realised he was holding his breath. What did he expect? A wolf dressed up as a grandma to jump out at them?

Instead he saw an open-plan area that brought the words *cosy*, *intimate* and *snug* to mind. Timber walls were decked with bright, vivid textiles and prints, there was a purple two-seater sofa, a fireplace piled with freshly chopped logs, a circular rustic pine table. Bright light flooded through the floor-to-ceiling window that looked out onto the crisp snow-covered garden. One corner of the room showcased an abundant Christmas tree decorated with beautifully crafted wooden decorations interspersed with red baubles.

'This is…dreamy…' Ruby said as she headed over to the table. 'Hey! Look! It's a hamper. Christmas coffee… Gingerbread… Nougat… Champagne…' Picking up a card, she twirled to face him. 'The larder and fridge are stocked with supplies as well.'

Okay, Ruby loved it, and for one disorientating second the look of wonder on her face made Ethan want to give her whatever she wanted.

A sudden sense that he was losing control sent an unfamiliar swirl of panic through his gut, caused him to strive for practicality. One swift glance took in the kitchen area, tiled and warm with pine and pottery, and another door through which he glimpsed a washing machine and a shower room. Which left…

'Oh!' Ruby gasped. 'Look! The ladder must lead up to the next storey. It's like a scene from *Heidi*.'

If there was a hayloft up there he would definitely sue the travel agent.

Ruby headed towards the ladder and started to climb, her long dark ponytail swinging a jaunty rhythm, her pert denim-clad bottom snagging his gaze.

Jeez. Get a grip, Ethan. They were in enough trouble.

Ruby stepped forward from the ladder-top and gazed around the cosy confines of the bedroom. The view from the window pulled her across the floor. Mountains sculpted the horizon, almost impossible in their precipitous snow-crested magnificence. A miracle of nature, of strata and formations that had resulted in a strength and enormity that dazzled— added to the swirl of emotions that pulsed through her. It was as if the chalet had indeed exerted some kind of Christmas spell over her.

Made her forget that this was a business trip, that any glimmer of attraction between them was impossible. Instead all that mattered to her was the fact that this place reeked of romance, oozed intimacy from every wooden beam and panel.

So much so that she couldn't think straight: images waltzed and corkscrewed through her mind. Cast her as the princess and Ethan as the knight in spotless armour. Setting the scene as the place where they would…

Her gaze plunged to the snug double bed, with its patterned quilt and simple wooden headboard. More vivid pictures tangled in her imagination: herself snuggled up to Ethan, falling asleep in dappled moonlight, warm and safe from the bitter cold outside, seduced into wakefulness by the trail of his fingers on her skin…

'On my way up.'

The sound of Ethan's voice was like an ice bucket of reality. What was the matter with her? Panic knotted her tummy as she leapt across the room to an interconnecting door and wrenched it open.

She swung round as Ethan mounted the ladder, willed her heart-rate to slow down, ordered her brain to leave the mushy fantasy world it had stupidly decided to inhabit. She should never have fallen asleep in the car. Falling asleep on a motorway and waking up in fairyland had obviously decimated her brain cells.

'The bedrooms…' she said.

Talk about a statement of the obvious.

He crossed the mezzanine floor and poked his head into the second room, so close that she had to close her eyes to combat the urge to touch him, to inhale his clean sandalwood scent. Whatever influence this place exerted had to be shaken off.

Holding her tummy in, she sidled past him towards the ladder-top.

'It's tiny,' Ethan said. 'It's for children. It's only got a minuscule bunk bed in it. That decides it. We can't stay here.'

A glitter of relief flecked his eyes and she clocked the almost imperceptible sag of those broad shoulders.

Ruby knew it was wrong, but the knowledge that Ethan Caversham was worried about staying here with her triggered a feminine satisfaction.

The fact that she had managed to breach the professional wall he'd built up since that near-kiss prompted her to step forward.

'I wouldn't mind sleeping in there. There's no way you could manoeuvre your way into the room, let alone the bed. But I'll be fine. I'm flexible.'

Unable to help herself, she gave a little shimmy to demonstrate the point and his jaw clenched again. *Whoa.* Probably best not to bite off more than she could nibble. But this chalet called to something deep inside her. It was a magical place, made for dreams, and even though she knew dreams were a fallacy surely there could be no harm in two days of magic? It was Christmas, for crying out loud.

'I think we should stay here. I mean, it's quirky—it's different. Maybe you could build a resort with places like this. Plus, it's a good place to work. No distractions.'

Bwa-ha-ha-ha! went her hormones as they rolled on the floor with mirth. As a small voice shrieked in the dark recesses of her brain, pointed out that all those diversions she'd dissed would have equalled an effective chaperon service.

'I'd like to stay here, but if you think it's too difficult…'

Too late it occurred to her that Ethan had never been able to resist a challenge. His eyebrows rose and suddenly the room seemed even smaller.

'So you want to stay here?'

'Yup.'

Determination solidified inside her—her ill-advised hormones would *not* govern her actions. This place was magical, and magical was what she wanted. Not just for herself, but for Ethan as well. Surely even his cynicism, his determination to treat Christmas as just another day, wouldn't be proof against this chalet?

He gave so much—wanted to make a difference in the lives of Max and Tara and others teens like them. Maybe it was time someone tried to make a difference for Ethan. That darkness she'd sensed inside him a decade ago—the darkness that still remained despite the aura of success—she wanted to change that, to lighten him up with some magic. How could that be wrong?

That small, insistent voice at the back of her mind clamoured to be heard—warned her that he hadn't wanted her help ten years before and he didn't want it now. It was advice she knew she should heed—she didn't know how to change people...never had, never would. So she should back off. Instead she met his gaze.

'Yes,' she repeated. 'I do want to stay here.'

Two days. It couldn't harm.

His broad shoulders lifted. 'Then so be it.'

The enormity of her own stupidity nearly overcame her. 'Fabulous,' she squeaked. 'So let's go and sample some of that Christmas coffee and gingerbread.'

And get out of the bedroom.

Repeating the mantra 'We are professional' under her breath, Ruby busied herself in the small kitchen area. Focused on the beautifully crafted pottery and the blue and white ceramic tiles as she made coffee. Inhaled its nutty roasted aroma and hoped it would defuse her disastrous awareness of Ethan.

Tray loaded, she headed to the lounge area. Flames crackled in the hearth and the sweet spicy scent of the logs infused the air.

Pouring out the coffee, handing out the gingerbread and lowering herself warily onto the sofa to avoid any form of thigh-to-thigh contact consumed all of five minutes.

The search for conversation turned out to be problematic. Ridiculous. Over the past days she and Ethan had spent hours in comfortable silence. Unfortunately right now comfort had legged it over the horizon into the alpine peaks.

Next to her Ethan shifted; she sipped her coffee as the silence stretched on.

This was madness—what had she been thinking? The ideal solution would have been to have let Ethan move them out of here. *Here* was the sort of place where couples came on honeymoon, cuddled in front of the flickering logs and cooed sweet nothings. Or the sort of place for a family holiday—a place where kids could build snow-men in the garden and sleep in that storybook bunk bed.

This must be anathema to Ethan, and yet he'd agreed to remain here. So the least she could do was come up with some conversation. A sideways glance noted that he looked brooding, one hand drumming on his knee almost as if he were wait-ing for something. Conversation, presumably.

'So, if you go ahead here would you set up your own ski school, complete with equipment hire and guides? Or use an existing school and arrange for some sort of commission?'

'They are both options I'll consider. It depends.'

That seemed to cover that. She reached out for another piece of the spicy gingerbread—oh, so aware of the jiggling of Ethan's leg, the tap-tap of his foot on the wooden floor. Silence reigned until Ethan put his coffee cup down with a clunk just as a jingling noise came from outside.

Turning, he cleared his throat. 'Right on time,' he declared, with a glance at his watch.

'What is?'

'Look out of the window.' Rising, he gave a sudden smile, an odd mix of relief and trepidation in the tipping of his lips.

Despite the temptation to absorb the impact of that smile, she unsnagged her gaze from his mouth, rose to her feet and headed for the expanse of glass.

The breath cascaded from her lungs—outside on the snow-laden road was a horse-drawn carriage. Not any old carriage, either—this one was in the style of a sleigh, complete with large red and black wheels and a fur-hooded roof. The sturdy brown horse was adorned with a festive bridle, resplendent with images of Father Christmas, and a blanket in deep red and green. The driver was bundled in coats and a high fur hat and lifted a hand in greeting.

'It's amazing...' Ruby breathed as she turned to Ethan.

'I thought you might like it,' he said, almost abruptly.

'I don't just like it. I love it! Thank you.'

For a second that seemed infinite he met her gaze and something flickered in his eyes—only to be doused as he scrubbed a hand over his jaw.

'I thought it would have mass appeal if I were

to offer high-end romantic Christmas breaks in the Alps.'

Wow—he couldn't have made it clearer that this wasn't personal. Hurt flashed across her ribcage… until she registered the slight croakiness to his tone, as if he were forcing the words out. She didn't believe him. Ethan had done this for *her*—had chosen this particular activity with her in mind—she knew it.

For heaven's sake.

She had to get a grip. Of course she didn't know it—it was another case of believing what she wanted to believe. Just as she'd believed her parents would change—had taken any stray kind word and built it up into a pointless dream. Just as she'd trusted that Gary and Steve and Hugh would change for her. Each and every time she had been blind and foolish.

Not any more.

'Let's get our coats.'

Curse words streamed through Ethan's brain—talk about acting like a class-A schmuck. What was he trying to prove? So what if he had chosen the itinerary with Ruby in mind? The whole point had been to give her a magical Christmas. To palliate the hurt of her Christmases Past—to do for her what she had done for Tara and Max and all those teenagers. There was nothing wrong with that—and yet panic continued to churn in his gut.

Deal with it, Ethan.

Sure, the last time Christmas had been magical for him had been when Tanya was alive. That magic hadn't stopped his sister from leaving this life scant months later. But that had zip to do with Ruby, and he wouldn't let his own past ruin this day for her.

'Wait!'

Ruby swivelled round on one booted foot, her poise back in place, her initial happiness and subsequent hurt both erased.

'Yes?'

'I apologise. I'm not good at this whole Christmas scenario, but I don't want this to be awkward. I want you to enjoy the ride and the itinerary and...'

And he wanted to kiss her so badly his lips tingled and his hands ached with the need to reach out for her. Somehow a kiss would show her what he meant when words seemed to have deserted his tongue...

Somehow he needed to get with it and recall Ethan Caversham, man-in-control, to the building.

'So how about we get this carriage on the road?'

Her gorgeous lips turned up in a smile so sweet that he knew she had intuitively understood what he meant even if he didn't.

'It's a plan. But first maybe this is the right time for me to give you your Christmas gifts.'

Surprise slammed into him. 'You bought me gifts?'

'No need to sound so shocked. Yes, I did. Hang on.' Anticipation etched her features as she walked over to her case. 'This one I bought ages ago. I was going to leave it at the castle for you to find. And this one was an impulse buy at the airport.'

'Thank you.'

In truth he had no idea what to say—he couldn't remember the last time he had been on the receiving end of a personal gift. His lips twisted in a rueful smile—in a sense he was still on a par with Max and Tara, *et al.*

Slipping a hand into his pocket, he retrieved his present for Ruby and sudden trepidation shot through his nerves. 'Here's yours. Ladies first.'

'Oh… You didn't have to. I know you don't really believe in Christmas.'

Ethan shrugged. 'I…I thought that…seeing how much effort you put into the teens' gifts…the least I could do was—' He broke off. He was doing it again. 'I wanted to.'

He had wanted Ruby to have a present that someone had thought about. Okay. Make that agonised over. How long had he spent in that stupid jewellery shop? Irritation caused his fingers to drum on his thigh as he felt his heart thud faster—he wanted her to like it way too much.

A yearning to see her eyes light up banded his chest as she carefully unwrapped the green embossed paper, held the dark blue jewellery box and then snapped it open and gasped, her lips forming a perfect O of wonder.

The pendant glittered, diamonds on white gold, shaped into an exquisite simple star. When he'd seen it an image of Ruby as she'd handed him the star to adorn the Christmas tree had popped into his mind.

'Ethan. I…I…can't accept this. It's not right. It's…'

'It's yours.'

Though by 'not right' maybe she meant she didn't like it…

An image of his mother that terrible first Christmas after Tanya's death flashed across his mind. Her wooden expression as she opened his gifts. The sear of knowledge that he'd got it wrong. That without Tanya he meant nothing to her, couldn't get it right. All those hours spent agonising for naught.

Maybe he should have learnt—stuck to something generic for Ruby. Better yet, he should have given her a Christmas bonus—a cheque, a banker's draft. Going personal had been a mistake. Ethan Caversham didn't do personal.

'You can exchange it if need be.'

'Exchange it?' she echoed. 'Why would I do that? It's beautiful. I meant it's too much.'

'It's a gift, Ruby.' It occurred to him that she was no more used to gifts than he was. 'I want you to have it.'

'Then thank you.'

As she took it from the box he thought for an instant that she would ask his help to put it on. Relief warred with disappointment when she lifted it herself—the thought of his fingers brushing the sensitive skin of her neck had strummed a jolt of pure desire through him.

'Now open yours.'

An absurd sense of excitement threaded his gut

as he unwrapped the first gift, the bright paper covered in images of Father Christmas bringing a smile to his lips. It was a smile that grew as warmth touched his chest.

In his hands was a painting of Caversham Castle. The artist had captured the sheer brooding history of the craggy mound of medieval stone, imposing and grand, made to defend and dominate the landscape.

'It's perfect. Thank you.'

'Open the next one.' A small frown creased her forehead. 'Like I said, this was an impulse buy and if you don't like it I won't be offended...'

As he pulled the jumper out of its silver wrapping paper a chuckle fell from his lips. 'A Christmas jumper.' A cable knit in dark blue, it was patterned with reindeer. 'It's inspired—and what better time to wear it?'

'You mean it?'

Surprise and a smile illuminated her face, and for one heartbeat full of exhilaration he nearly succumbed to the temptation to sweep her into his arms and kiss her.

No! There was personal and there was *personal*.

Instead he tugged the jumper over his head 'Of course. Now, let's go!'

A few minutes later and they were all layered up. Once outside, Ethan sucked in the cold air; welcomed the hit to his lungs and brain. Perhaps the cold would freeze some sense into him.

CHAPTER ELEVEN

RUBY STOLE A sideways glance at Ethan and tried to confine the tornado of her thoughts. *Yeah, right.* Containment continued to elude her, effectively held at bay by the sheer nearness of Ethan as they settled under the heap of blankets on the carriage seat. Ruby clenched her jaw—she would not even contemplate the word snuggle.

Somehow she had to keep perspective, had to chillax and not read more into Ethan's actions than there was. After all, she had earned a diploma in that. Yes, he had bought her a beautiful Christmas gift—instinctively her hand rose to touch the diamond pendant—but that was because Ethan was a good man who tried to give people second chances.

No doubt he had simply wanted to do for her what he had wanted to do for all those troubled teenagers. In fact he had practically said so…so there was no point to this continued analysis.

Time instead to concentrate on the beauty of

her surroundings, which was enough to catch the breath in her throat. The ground was covered in snow, as if someone had taken the time to weave a thick white duvet to cover the landscape and then sprinkled the bare branches of the trees with a dazzling glitter. It was beautiful—glorious—magical. The silence was broken only by the chime of the horse's bells, the huff of his breath and the crunch of his hooves in the snow.

'This is beyond incredible,' she murmured with a sideways glance.

Ethan's expression was unreadable, but the vibe she got from him was edgy—as if he too battled complicated thoughts.

Her words caused him to blink and give a small shake of his head. 'I'm glad you're enjoying it,' he said. 'Not too cold?'

'Nope. The last time I saw snow was in London, and it had turned to slush before I could truly appreciate its beauty. This is spectacular.'

Now a genuine smile touched his lips as his gaze rested on her expression. 'I hope you'll like the next item on our agenda.'

'Which is…?'

'Sledging.'

'For real?'

Excitement fizzed inside her and collided with a pang of emotion as a memory jolted her brain. Years and years ago she'd taken her siblings out into the snow. She'd carried Edie, who hadn't been able to walk yet, Philippa had toddled beside her and Tom, aged just four, had raced ahead with a joyous whoop. They hadn't gone far, just to a local park to watch the children sledge.

How she had yearned to have a go. But there had been no sledge, and she hadn't wanted to draw attention to themselves. But it had still been a good day—they had made a snowman, thrown some snowballs, before Ruby had realised that there were some adults clearly wondering why they were unaccompanied and she'd quickly herded her siblings together and left.

'Is that okay?' A small frown touched Ethan's face as he studied her expression and she did her best to erase the hint of wistfulness, the shadow of memory from her face.

'It's better than okay. I've never sledged before and I would absolutely love to.'

Ruby let the memory go with the silent hope that her siblings had had plenty of opportunity to sledge with their new family. Allowed the fizz of excitement to take ascendancy.

Minutes later the carriage drew to a halt and Ethan helped her alight. 'Here we are. It's a resort, but we have passes.'

They lingered for a moment to thank the driver and pat the horse, and then she turned and once again the scenery caused the breath to whoosh from her lungs. Snow glistened in the distant trees of the forest and crunched underfoot, thick and soft all at the same time—the way she had imagined stepping on clouds would be as a child.

They entered the resort and headed to the sledge hire desk.

The woman behind the counter smiled. 'Would you like a paret, a disc or a toboggan?'

Ruby stared at the options. 'I'll go for a toboggan.' On the basis that it looked the safest. The paret looked to be a mixture of a tricycle without wheels and a stool, and the disc looked as if it might well career round and round out of control. As that was her current mental state, there was no point adding a physical element.

The woman smiled. 'I promise they are all safe, *mademoiselle*. They are designed to be safe for children as well as adults.'

'I'll try the paret,' Ethan said.

Ruby narrowed her eyes. 'Show-off.'

That garnered a smile. 'Think of it as research. It's occurred to me that I could offer moonlit paret sledging as a part of a holiday package.'

They exited the building and she inhaled the tang of snow and pine, absorbed the bustle of people and the sound of laughter. Took courage from the happy vibe.

Until they reached the top of the slope.

'Um…' Ruby peered over the edge.

Suddenly the snow was reminiscent of clouds only in the way that if you tried to walk on a cloud you would plummet downwards. The ground was a turreted mass of white, under which surely there would lurk hidden dangers.

'You worried?'

Daft. She was being daft. This was an official slope, suitable for tiny kids. All she needed to do was look around again and observe them.

Her heart gave a sudden thump. Just a few feet away a mother with a baby in a sling helped two children get onto a sledge. A dark-haired boy and a younger little girl with blonde curls. The world seemed to fall into slow motion and for an absurd second she nearly ran towards them—until common sense drummed its beat.

That wasn't Tom and Philippa. Tom would be

twenty now, and Philippa nineteen. Even if they were here she wouldn't recognise them. They were adults.

For a second, loss shredded her insides.

'Ruby?' Ethan's rich voice held a question and a heap of concern.

For a mad minute she wanted to tell him the truth, in the hope that he could soothe the pain.

With muscle-aching effort she pulled herself together. Confiding in Ethan would only add to the intimacy she was trying to fight. In any case Ethan didn't welcome emotional intensity; he hadn't ten years before and he wouldn't now.

'I'm fine. Just chicken, I guess. Why don't you show me how it's done?'

'No. You look like you've seen a ghost. We're going to the café.'

'I...'

'No arguments. First rule of snow sport. You don't do it unless you're focused.'

Maybe he was right. Either way he wasn't taking no for an answer and willy-nilly Ruby followed him towards the café.

Ethan held the café door open. The smell of coffee jumbled up with the aromas of vanilla and almond and Christmas spices. Carols filled the air with a choral hum—a festive backdrop to the chatter of families and the clink-clank of cutlery. Usually the scents would have triggered a smile, but Ruby seemed enmeshed in thought.

Even an almond croissant and hot chocolate didn't bring more than a perfunctory smile to her face.

'You want to talk about it?' Even as he spoke the words he knew it was a foolhardy query. The invitation to confide, to *share*, was not one he would ever make as a rule. Panic threatened—an echo of a decade ago. He was letting her get too close. But how could he help it? When she looked to be in such pain, with her usual vividness drained? He wanted to help, to make it better for her.

If he had any sense he would never have let things get to this point—maybe he should have let history repeat itself and cut and run.

Chill, Ethan.

Time to remember that he was ten years older now, ten years wiser, and this time he would be able to control the situation. There could be no danger in an offer of support and it would be an impossibility to withhold that support.

'If you want to talk I'm here.'

Her eyes met his with a hint of surprise, palpable hesitation, and a small determined shake of her head. 'It's Christmas. You've gone to all this trouble. I'm sorry to be a Debbie Downer.'

'You aren't. I promise. Ruby, we both know that Christmas can be an emotive time for people with difficult pasts. Talk to me. I know your childhood Christmases were grim. Maybe I can dilute some of your tainted memories.'

One more heartbeat of a pause and then she exhaled. Picked up the steaming mug of hot chocolate and cradled it, her eyes wide. 'I guess for a moment out there the past arrived from nowhere and knocked me for a half-dozen. Those children on the sledge next to us… For an instant they reminded me of my younger brother and sisters.'

The words registered in his brain—generated a host of questions. If Ruby had siblings where were they now? Why did the memory of them haunt her?

Her gloved hand pushed a tendril of hair from her face and she sighed. The noise escaped into the chatter-tinged air with the sound of age-old sorrow and weariness.

'Tom, Edie and Philippa,' she continued. 'I told you my parents were addicts. One of the ways they funded their addictions was via benefits. The more children they had, the more money they got. I was the oldest, then Tom, Philippa and Edie. I was six when Tom was born, and I can still remember the awe I felt when I first saw him—such a tiny scrap of humanity. I felt welded to him. Same with the girls. All I wanted was for us to stay together as a family, and I vowed I would do whatever it took. Mum and Dad told me that it was up to me—that they couldn't do it so I had to be strong. I had to be responsible. I had to lie to social workers and school teachers. Had to make sure everyone believed we were a happy family.'

Ethan's chest constricted at the sight of her face, whiter than the snow that glittered and glinted outside. He could picture a much younger Ruby, her expression oh, so serious, tucking an unruly curl of dark hair behind her ear as she concentrated on changing a nappy or manoeuvred a heavy pan of water onto the hob.

'That must have been tough,' he said softly.

'It was and it wasn't. I loved them all so much, you see—and I told myself that Mum and Dad loved us really. But the cold hard truth is that they used us. More fool me for ever thinking otherwise. Even after it all went wrong, when I screwed it up, for ages I still kidded myself that they loved me.'

'What happened?'

'I couldn't hold up the façade and it crumbled down. We were whisked away into care. They couldn't find a carer to take all four of us so we were split up. We went from being a family unit to having visits in a social worker's office once a week if we were lucky.'

'That must have been beyond terrible.'

'It was.'

Her words were flat and in that moment he knew that it had been unfathomably horrific.

'I fought for us to be placed together, or at least near each other. But nothing I said made any difference. The social workers said that we were better off like that than with our parents. But it didn't seem that way to me. Sometimes I even pictured my parents missing us so much that they would turn over a new leaf and we'd all go back to them.'

She laughed—the noise devoid of mirth.

'I take it that didn't happen?'

'Nope. They turned up to see me once—stoned and drunk—hurled abuse at me and the social worker ended the meeting. I've never seen them again. No idea if they are alive or dead.'

He placed his hand over hers, wished he could find words to convey his feelings.

'Time went—and one day a social worker came and told me she had good news. An adoptive family had been found, but they would only take three children—Tom, Edie and Philippa. I was too old and too difficult. I'd been acting out, and they figured it would be bad for the others if I was placed with them.'

She paused, her blue eyes wide and unfocused, as if she had teleported through time to relive the moment.

'The social worker explained that if they waited, kept trying to find someone to take all of us, it might end up that none of us got adopted—or that Tom, Edie and Philippa would end up separated. She promised me there would still be contact. I'd still see them. But it didn't go down like that. Tom Edie and Philippa moved in with their new family and I was told there would be no contact whilst they settled in. I fought it—I went on and on to the carers, to the social workers. They told me I had to wait. That I was being selfish. Then one day I decided to take matters in my own hands.

I bunked off and went to their school. I was so desperate to see if they were okay. That's all I'd ever done, you see.'

Her hands gripped the mug of hot chocolate so hard he leant over and prised her fingers free, retained her hand in his grasp. He could envisage her so clearly; frantic and determined, fuelled by a love that gave her the strength to do anything for the sake of her siblings.

'It was the end of school—I saw them run out to a woman who I knew must be their new mum. She looked so pretty, and like she adored them, and they looked so happy. It just needed Mary Poppins to make it complete. Not me.'

'Oh, jeez, Ruby...'

What could he say? What could he do to fix this? To mend the void that echoed from her voice? Helplessness gnawed at his insides and he did the only thing he could. Moved his chair round the table in the hope that his body, his presence, would offer some comfort.

'After I saw that I knew what I needed to do. I told the social worker that I didn't want to see my siblings for a while. That I understood it was better for them to integrate into their new family. Eventually, with a social worker's approval,

I wrote them a letter to tell them I loved them but a clean break was better for all of us. I knew it was right—my presence in their lives would only make everyone feel bad. Their new family would feel bad for not being able to take me, and Tom and Edie and Philippa's loyalty would be divided. That wouldn't have been good for them. So I decided there and then that I would try and be happy for them.'

Her slim shoulders lifted.

'And I *am* happy for them. But occasionally I still miss them so much it hurts.'

A solitary tear seeped from her eye and he reached out and caught it on his thumb. The moisture glistened on the pad of his glove and he pulled her into his arms.

'It's okay, Ruby. Cry it out.'

Her body tensed and he rubbed her back in a gentle circular motion. Felt her relax as she snuggled into his chest and wept. From somewhere he found soothing words as he rested his cheek on the silkiness of her hair. He realised he couldn't remember a time when he had done this. Offered comfort. Oh he'd tried with his mother, after Tanya, but she'd pushed him away, her whole body stiff with grief. Her eyes had told him what she had later confirmed in words—the wish that it had been him who had died rather than his sister.

He pushed the thoughts away—right now it was all about Ruby. His past couldn't be changed or fixed—his mother had no wish to mend fences in any way. Tracey Caversham wouldn't even take his money, let alone any affection. But he was grateful that Ruby seemed to derive some comfort from his actions.

After a while she placed her palms on his chest and gently pushed herself upright. 'Phew,' she said as she looked up at him, tear-swept eyes glistening. 'I'm sorry. What you said was so beautiful, and suddenly I could see them so vividly. Memories deluged me and turned me into a watering pot.'

'There's no need to apologise. At all. I'm glad you told me. Tell me more about them. About Tom, Edie and Philippa.'

So she did, and as she spoke he could visualise the energetic, dark-haired Tom, with his cheeky grin, see the chatterbox Philippa with her blonde ringlets and quiet, straight-haired Edie who sucked her thumb.

When she'd stopped speaking Ruby squeezed his hands. 'Thank you. Mostly I try to leave the past in the past. But sharing the good memories has made the bad memories easier to bear. I feel lighter. Thank you, Ethan—and I mean that. If you ever want to talk I'm here for you.'

Her words triggered a strange reaction—for a second he allowed himself to ponder that scenario. Tried to picture the concept of sharing. Sharing with Ruby the way his mother's face had always twisted at the sight of him, the continued rain of comments as to how he reminded her of his dad. How Tanya had shielded him with her love, but how that shield had been tragically removed by her suicide. His terrible grief and its aftermath. How spectacularly he had let his mother down and the devastating consequences.

Discomfort rippled in his gut, along with a healthy dose of denial, and he felt his lips curl with distaste. *Not happening.* If there was one thing his past had taught him it was the need to control emotion—all the release of it could achieve was pain. If he had only retained control after Tanya's death then he wouldn't have walked the road that had led to his mother handing him over to social services. To confide in Ruby would open up an emotional vortex and that was not going to happen.

So… 'I'll bear it in mind,' he said as he pushed her plate towards her. 'So what now?'

Ruby picked up the almond croissant. 'I'd like to eat this, and then—if it's okay with you—I'd still like to sledge.'

'Then that's the plan.'

It truly felt as if a bulk had been hefted from her very soul. The sadness was still there, but more manageable. As they exited the café the snow seemed even brighter, and now the sight of children filled her with a sense of hope and determination. Because one day she would adopt, and she vowed that she would take her children sledging.

A sideways glance at Ethan filled her with relief—his blue-grey eyes rested on her with warmth, but not a hint of pity, and she honoured him for that. For his innate realisation that pity would be anathema to her.

There was a bond between them now—she could see it shimmer in the air between them. They had both pulled themselves from the gutter and survived events that had had the potential to destroy. That was worthy of admiration—not pity. But she knew she felt more than admiration, and she needed to be careful. Because right now that gooey warmth had multiplied, and instead of being mortified at having wept all over him she felt energised...awash with dangerous feelings of intimacy. An intimacy he would abhor.

Sure, he had just proved himself capable of emotional understanding, but his withdrawal at the thought of sharing his own past had been crystal-clear.

She had to rein it in. Her goals and Ethan's goals were as far apart as it was possible to be. Ethan wanted to sit in his un-rocked boat on his own— he wanted a life alone—and she wanted as many children as she could manage. So her best hope was that she and Ethan could become friends.

Yet right now she wanted more...couldn't help herself. The tug of attraction, the tug of emotion, the tug towards him in general asserted a magnetism she somehow had to control. Because there couldn't be anything else, and she couldn't let herself fall headlong for yet another unsuitable man. Another man who would not or could not change his lifestyle for her.

Instead it would be better to focus on what she could share with Ethan—like this wonderful Christmas Day he had given her. Maybe she needed to focus on a headlong ride on a sledge...

A peek down the slope and she felt a surge of anticipation.

'Take it away, maestro,' she said.

His smile was the genuine article—it lit his grey-blue eyes and her tummy clenched in response.

'As you wish,' he said, and he turned, dropped down onto the disc sledge and launched himself down the slope. Tore down the slope, swerved and manoeuvred, flew over the snow.

Once at the bottom he looked up and gave her the thumbs-up sign before beginning his ascent. She watched him climb back up, legs strong and body lithe. What was it about him that made him stand out? Maybe his aura—one that meant she would be able to spot him anywhere in the world.

'There—see. Easy.'

Ruby looked down at the toboggan doubtfully. 'I'm still not convinced I won't fall off.'

'It's all about balance.'

'Very Zen...'

His chuckle caught on the crisp breeze, and unlocked something inside her. The sight of his smile and the tang of snow made her breath catch, made her heart hop, skip and jump. and she felt her lips tilt into a grin.

'Zen or not, you are going down that slope, Ruby. We'll go together. This is one childish dream that you *will* fulfil. Come on. Sit. I'll fit in behind you.'

Huh?

She squatted, placed the plastic toboggan on the snow and wriggled on, intensely aware of him as he lowered himself behind her. This was daft— they were both in Eskimo-level layers of clothing on a populated slope—not sunbathing on an isolated beach in bikini and trunks.

Ethan placed one arm round her waist and she swallowed her small gasp. His touch defied physics, felt electric through all the layers.

'So all you have to do to steer is use this stick on the side, or your hands or feet.'

Was it her imagination or was his voice deeper than normal—the sort of deep that made her think of dark chocolate with a hint of ginger and spicy mulled wine? Panic mixed with a tummy-tingle of need.

Do something, Ruby.

'Let's go!'

They took off, skimmed over the snow. Exhilaration heated her veins as she let go, with no time to think or analyse or worry. She existed in the second, fuelled by adrenalin and sheer excitement as the world flew by until they reached the base and glided to a stop.

Pure elation frothed inside her as she shifted to look up at Ethan. 'That was incredible. Like an out-of-body experience.'

Ruby stared at him. He looked…utterly gorgeous. And in this mood of sheer instinct she knew with a blind, horrible clarity that she wanted him to kiss her. That the tingles that coursed through her body were no longer due to her sledging experience. This attraction existed. No—it did more than that. Right now it burned…just like his gaze that was focused on her parted lips.

His pupils darkened; desire flared.

'Ethan…?'

The question whispered across the snow-tinged air. Her heart pounded in her ribcage as her lips parted and she twisted round, propelled by an instinct older than time, her body no longer at home to the voice of reason.

CHAPTER TWELVE

ETHAN COULDN'T TEAR his gaze from her—she was so incredibly beautiful. Her cheeks flushed from the cold, her entire face animated by desire. And, heaven help him, he couldn't help himself—couldn't stop himself.

Leaning forward, he covered her lush lips with his own as precipitous need overcame all capacity for thought. It felt so right. He could taste Ruby—the tang of almond with a hint of chocolate. Her lips, cold at first, heated up and she gave a small mewl. The sound triggered a further yearning for more and he pushed his fingers under the hood of her parka, tangled his fingers in the silk of her hair. Her lips parted and her tongue touched his in a tentative flick. And he was lost in a desire to block out the world and kiss her until…

Until what?

The knowledge that the universe could not be ignored was one he carried with him every second of the day; there were always consequences.

Problem was at this instant he couldn't care less—which was dangerous beyond belief. He mustn't let her close. For both their sakes. Ruby wanted a family and she deserved to have that—she might believe now that she wanted single parenthood, but he hoped that one day she would find love with a man who could give her everything she deserved. Ethan was not that man—and he would not mess with her head.

With a supreme effort of will he pulled back and for a long second they gazed at each other, puffs of breath mingling in the cold.

'I…' Her voice trailed off as she lifted her fingers to her lips again. As if they stung in sheer frustration.

Well he could empathise with that. All of him was tingling with spikes of unfulfilled need.

'I…um…what now?'

'I don't know.'

What could he say? There was no point trying to dismiss what had happened. That kiss had been off the Richter scale and it had changed everything. Which was a problem.

'But I apologise.' From somewhere he pulled a smile—this Christmas Day would *not* be ruined by his stupidity. 'We need to forget that happened. And whilst we try to do that let's keep sledging.'

Truth be told, he couldn't think what else to do. The alternative was to hotfoot it back to the chalet and haul her into the bedroom.

A silence, and then she essayed a small, determined nod. 'Okay,' she agreed. 'This is such an amazing place to be, and I am having a wonderful Christmas Day, so don't apologise. We can chalk it up to an inevitable moment of foolishness.'

To his surprise there was no awkwardness in the next few hours—Ruby took to the snow like the proverbial duck to water, and swerved and dipped and dived over the slopes. They raced each other and laughed over the results, argued with mock ferocity over a handicap system, and sledged until dusk hit.

'Time for the next stop,' Ethan said. 'Gaston should be back with the carriage and then it's time for Christmas drinks and dinner in town.'

The knowledge was a relief, because despite all his efforts the air still hummed with the undercurrent of attraction and they needed time before they returned to the problematic fairy tale chalet, with its solitude and adjoining bedrooms.

'Great.' Ruby clapped her hands together to get rid of the last vestige of snow and leant with natural grace to pick up her toboggan.

The carriage journey into town was silent—but not a silence of an awkward or grim calibre. Ethan would have classed it as one infused with an undercurrent he wasn't sure he grasped. Every so often Ruby would glance at him with a sideways sweep, her eyes wide in thought as one finger curled a tendril of dark hair that escaped from her red bobble hat.

And then the horse came to a halt and they disembarked into the Christmas card scene of the Alpen town. The atmosphere was lively, and the artful array of high-end shops was combined with an olde-worlde charm.

'It's gorgeous…' Ruby breathed.

As was she.

They walked down the snow-dusted street, illuminated by the glow of lights from the multitude of bars and restaurants and the twinkle of lights that decked the air. Next to him Ruby had subsided back into silence. She broke it with a quick look up at him.

'Where are we having dinner?'

'A Michelin-starred restaurant owned by the

resort. We're a bit early, but we can have a drink before.'

'How about in here?' she suggested, stopping outside a bar that resembled an old coaching inn.

'Sure.'

They stepped over the threshold into the warmth of the bar. Chatter in a variety of languages mingled with universal laughter and the chink and rattle of glasses and cutlery. The aroma of fondue and beer was mixed with the tang of snow.

'What would you like?'

'A small glass of white wine, please.' Ruby eyed him with something very near speculation as she tugged her bobble hat off.

'Coming right up.' He shrugged out of his jacket and dropped it on the back of a chair whilst she seated herself at the round wooden table. As he headed through the throng to the bar he was aware of her eyes as they followed his progress.

Minutes later he returned and placed her wine and his tankard of beer on the table. He sat down and surveyed her thoughtful expression. Something had shifted and he wasn't sure what it was. The idea that they were on the brink of new territory sent a conflict of anticipation and panic to his synapses.

Ruby lifted her glass. 'To us. And how far we've come.'

Her words seemed imbued with meaning. The crowd and the hum of conversation seemed to fade, to leave only Ruby and himself. Perhaps he should make a stalwart attempt to pull the conversation round to work, but the idea refused to be translated into words.

The moment they had avoided so dextrously refused to be ignored any longer. That kiss—the mammoth in the room—was sitting right next to them, drink in hand. All he could think about was how her lips had felt, the wonder and the beauty and the sheer pleasure of that kiss. A kiss he'd waited a decade for…the desire he'd run from all those years ago. And now…

Ruby leant forward, her sapphire eyes sparkling as she tucked a stray tendril of hair behind her ear. 'I've been thinking, and I want…' Her cheeks flushed with a tinge of pink. 'I want…I want—' She broke off. 'Maybe it's better to start with what I don't want. I don't want a relationship with you. I don't want to climb into your boat or to rock it in any way whatsoever. My goal is adoption, and I will not let anything stand in my way.'

A pause whilst she sipped her drink.

'But I would like to explore this further. You and me. Just whilst we're here. Like a bubble of time between our pasts and our futures. I'd like to enjoy the now. With you. A two-night holiday fling. That's what you normally do, isn't it?'

No! It was an enormous effort to haul the syllable back. But instinct revolted, because Ethan knew that whatever happened between him and Ruby it didn't class with his usual liaisons.

'No.' The word was gentle. 'No, Ruby. You are different. If we do this I need you to know that.'

If they did this.

Ethan tried to think—when all he wanted to do was punch the air in triumph, sling Ruby over his shoulder caveman-style and get back to the chalet pronto. But he couldn't do that. Ruby had thought this through and he needed to do that as well.

Hours before he had ended their kiss because he had believed it was a bad idea—succumbing to emotion and impulse would land him in trouble. Worse, it could land *Ruby* in trouble, and he wouldn't let that happen. She'd been messed around enough by the men in her life— he wouldn't add to that.

'Ethan, I won't get hurt.'

Great. Clearly she could read him like a picture book.

'This is *my* idea. As soon as we get on the plane back home we revert to normal. Boss and employee. And we throw ourselves into making the ball a success. This will work.'

Her words held conviction and sense. Ruby did not want a relationship with him—she wanted a fling. There would be no further expectation, so he would not be messing with her head. Ruby wanted a family—he didn't. There could be no future. Her words.

For a scant second a warning bell clanged at the back of his brain—he didn't want to let Ruby close, remember? But Ethan wasn't in danger—how could he be? This was a fling—purely physical, no emotions on the table.

'Let's do it,' he said.

Ruby held her breath, giddy with sheer disbelief—had she really propositioned Ethan Caversham? *Yup*—she believed she had. For a scant second she wondered if she'd lost her mind. Yet if her sanity had gone walkabout she was in no hurry to get it back. Not when Ethan's eyes raked over her, glinting with a promise of fulfilment that sent shivers dancing up her spine.

'Let's go,' she said. 'Would you mind skipping dinner? I don't think I could eat a thing. But if you're hungry...'

Be quiet, Ruby. Before he changes his mind.

'I don't want dinner.'

His voice sent the tingle into acrobatic overdrive and sheer anticipation wobbled her legs as she slipped off the bar stool. As he encased her hand in his she knew her smile rivalled that of a plethora of Cheshire cats. This was all about the moment, and this moment felt fabulous, unrestricted by the past or the future.

Even the wait at the taxi stand, the journey back, felt alight with possibility—and then the magical glow of the chalet welcomed them.

Without releasing her hand Ethan manoeuvred the door open and tugged her straight across the lounge area.

Ruby disengaged her grasp to scramble up the ladder and into the bedroom. Now the reassurance of his touch had gone a sudden shyness threatened, caused her to circumnavigate the bed and approach the window.

The hairs on the back of her neck stood to at-

tention as she sensed his presence behind her, and
then his warmth enveloped her. His hands rested
on her shoulders and began to knead gently. Tension ebbed away as she gazed out at the garden,
where moonbeams danced on the birches and skittered in gleams on the duvet of snow.

Ethan swept her hair from her nape and she
gasped as his lips grazed the sensitive flesh. An
urge to see him overcame her, and as if he instinctively knew he stepped back and gently turned
her to face him.

'So beautiful...' he murmured, one thick finger
stroking her cheek.

His grey-blue eyes shone in the moon's illumination, the light played on the planes of his face
and emphasised their strength. Her heart melted
and ached and she reached up for him, greedy for
the devastation of his kiss.

It was a kiss that seemed to take up from where
they'd left off—only this time with the knowledge that there was more to come. There was no
need to think or analyse or worry, and that added
a sharp edge to a desire that dizzied her. Propelled by instinct, she gripped his shoulders and
Ethan lifted her effortlessly, so her legs wrapped
his waist and his hands cupped her bottom.

He carried her to the bed, their lips still locked, and Ruby moaned as he slid her down the hard length of his body before tumbling her onto the mattress.

Hours later Ruby opened her eyes, aware of an immense contentment that swathed her limbs in languorous satisfaction. For a long moment she lay and gazed up at the ceiling, cocooned under the weight of Ethan's arm, his dark brown head next to hers. A gentle shift and she could study his face, bathed in the streaks of dawn that slid through the slats of the shutters. Softer in sleep, yet still his features held a tautness—as if even in slumber he were loath to relinquish complete control.

A qualm tugged at her heart as it hopped, skipped and jumped. But there was nothing to worry about—she had decided that she wanted to grasp this opportunity, to live in the moment and just be herself. Because with Ethan that was who she could be—she'd shared her past and she'd shared her future. Now she wanted this time with him to explore their attraction.

Though somehow the theory no longer seemed so simple. Certain flaws had popped into her mind. These past hours had shown her an attraction that flamed with a heat she hadn't envisaged. But the fire would burn itself out. Though when fires burnt themselves out didn't they often leave a whole lot of collateral damage...?

His eyes opened and instantly focused—barely a fraction of a second between oblivion and awareness.

And she doused every qualm as his smile warmed her. She was being daft. They only had a day and a night left. Then it would be over. So what was the point of worry? It was not as if she had any intention of calling a halt to proceedings. Of not experiencing the wonder of the previous hours again...not falling asleep in the safe cocoon of his arms—the idea was unthinkable.

'Ruby? You okay?'

'Of course I am.'

Of course she was. *Jeez*. She really needed to work on her live-in-the-moment technique. The whole point was to enjoy each and every moment of the next twenty-four hours.

Twenty-four hours. *Tick-tock* went a metaphorical clock.

Concern lit his eyes and she summoned a smile. 'Just hungry. Guess it's time to eat. Not that I have a single regret for missing that Michelin-starred Christmas dinner.'

'Me neither. Our evening was spent in far more enjoyable ways. But now you mention it I am pretty hungry. I think we need to build up our strength,' he added with a wiggle of his eyebrows that made a giggle bubble up to the surface.

'And why would that be, Mr Caversham?'

Leaning over, he nuzzled her ear. 'In fact, perhaps I could muster up my last reserves of energy right now...'

'Hmm...' Desire sizzled through her with intoxicating speed—perhaps enjoying each and every moment would be a cinch after all.

An hour later he grinned lazily at her. 'Now would be a good time for breakfast.'

'How about I whip us up a brunch fondue?'

'Sounds perfect. I'll check our Boxing Day itinerary.'

'Okay. And thank you for a magical Christmas Day—the planned bits and the...the...' Her cheeks heated up.

'Impromptu night-time activities?' he supplied, with a wicked smile that curled her toes.

The morning hours swept by and she could almost see the magical motes of happiness fleck the air. Magic infused them both—brought laughter and warmth, enabled Ethan to dance round the kitchen disco-style whilst she sang along into a wooden spoon in lieu of a microphone.

Even the fondue worked—the mixture of Emmental, Gruyère and Comté provided a tang that burst onto their tastebuds, and the consistency of the bubbling cheese and wine was neither too thick nor too thin. Perfect for dunking cubes of baguette.

'Ruby, that was awesome. I am truly replete. Why don't you relax by the fire and I'll wash up?'

'You wash. I'll dry. You did help cook.'

'That's a generous interpretation of grating cheese.'

'You did an excellent job of stirring as well.'

Ruby looked over her shoulder as she carried their plates towards the kitchen area and glanced at the clock. A sudden sense of panic touched her. *Tick-tock*.

Stop it, Ruby.

This was an interlude—it couldn't go on for ever and she wouldn't want it to. Work was way too important, along with her goals and her future life. A future in which Ethan would only feature in a professional sense.

'Anyway, we'd best get this cleared up quick—the carriage will be back to take us into town for the Boxing Day market, followed by a mountain ascent.'

'Sounds brilliant.'

Maybe Ethan was right—the key was to keep moving, garner the maximum number of precious memories from this time capsule.

The hustle and bustle of the town square soothed her. It was littered with stalls, and the air was alight with chatter, wafting with a cluster of glorious scents. As she stood and inhaled the tang of gingerbread, the scent of the pine so evocative of the Christmas Day just gone, her qualms faded away along with the concern they had created.

This was all about a magical interlude and for once she was in control. There was no question of delusions or false dreams or hopes. This fling had been her idea, entered into with the knowledge that Ethan wouldn't change, and she was good with that.

She opened her eyes to find Ethan's grey-blue eyes fixed on her and she smiled at him, drank in the craggy features, the breadth of his shoulders, his aura of strength. Desire lodged deep in the hollow of her tummy—this freaking gorgeous man was hers. For now... And that was enough. For now she would live in the moment.

'This is such a wonderful place,' she said. 'I'd come on holiday for the market alone.'

The fresh produce was enough to make her taste-buds explode in anticipation. Cheeses abounded, bowls heaped with olives glistened, dried meats and *saucissons* hung in tempting displays.

'Shall I buy ingredients for dinner tonight?' she asked, the words so deliciously intimate. The idea of the evening ahead enticed her: cosy in the chalet, preparing dinner, a glass of wine, music in the background, smooth conversation, the exchange of a kiss here and there...

Purchases made, she espied the Christmas stalls, still piled high with festive adornments. Wooden gifts, bright wrapping paper, carved toys and gaudy sweets. Simple carved Christmas decorations, each one chunky and unique. One of the reindeer looked back at her, its antlers glistening in the afternoon sun.

Surprise laced her as Ethan picked it up and studied it. Then he nodded at the stallholder. 'I'll take one of each.'

'What are you doing? We did Christmas already. Anyway, I thought you weren't into decorations.'

'They're for you. To keep for your perfect Christmas. I know it'll happen for you.'

Tears prickled the back of her eyes. 'Thank you.'

A vision strobed in her mind. But it was wrong… Because there was Ethan, standing by a Christmas tree as he helped a small brown-haired boy hang the decorations. Around the other side of a tree a slightly older dark-haired girl was being helped by a teenager to thread a garland of tinsel.

Squeezing her nails into the palms of her hands, she erased the imaginary scene and shoved it firmly into her brain's 'Deleted' file. Time to concentrate on the moment, on the here and now. On the imposing grandeur of Mont Blanc as it towered over the town…on the fact that she was about to ascend a high mountain peak with this gorgeous man.

The stallholder handed her the bag and she smiled. 'They are perfect. Now, we had better get going—before we miss the ascent.'

CHAPTER THIRTEEN

ETHAN STRODE DOWN the street, an unfamiliar warmth heating his chest. It was as if this bubble of time theory had freed him to…to what? To *feel*? A soupçon of worry trickled through the fuzzy feel-good haze. Feelings netted nothing but pain and loss.

Chill.

Once they got on that plane in less than twenty-four hours everything would snap back to normal. Work would become paramount and all these strange feelings would dissipate.

'You okay?' she asked.

'I'm good.'

Without thought he took her hand in his and they made their way towards the ticket office. Picked up their tickets and joined the press of people in the gondola. When was the last time he had held someone's hand? Not since childhood, when he'd teetered along holding Tanya's hand.

The concept was strange, and for a moment he

stared down at their clasped hands before releasing Ruby's hand under the pretence of losing his balance. The motion was abrupt, and it left him with a strange sense of bereavement as he fixed his eyes on the view as they ascended the steep elevation.

Ruby too was silent, until they disembarked at very top, when she halted, her lips parted in a gasp that denoted sheer wonder. Ethan stared too. The incredible vista was one that emptied the lungs and constricted the throat. Panoramic didn't cover it.

They walked slowly across the terrace and Ruby hesitated as she approached the rail.

'You okay?' he asked. 'The altitude could be making you dizzy.'

'I do feel a little light-headed, but I think that's because I am awestruck.'

'Ditto.'

The snow-covered expanse stretched and stretched; the sky surrounded them in a cerulean blue cloak.

Ruby gestured towards the now far-distant town that looked as if it might be made from building bricks. 'Wow! Being up here, encompassed by Nature's might—it puts things into perspective.

We are here for such a minuscule slice of time compared to this universality. It makes me feel insignificant.'

'You could never be insignificant.'

Not this woman, with her determination, courage and her capacity to give.

She tugged her hat further down her head and he stepped closer to her to share his body warmth; the icy temperature permeated their thick padded layers.

'That's kind, Ethan, but it's not true. One day I hope I *will* be significant—help turn someone's life around. But until then...'

'No.' The idea that she believed herself insignificant did not sit well with him. 'You have already touched so many people's lives. Look at what you did for your brother and sisters.'

She shook her head. 'I did my best, but you know the saying—the road to hell is paved with good intentions. If I'd been stronger I wouldn't have shielded my parents for so long. I believed what they said—believed they would turn their lives around for us. So I lied, I pretended, but I was a fool. There were times when there wasn't enough food, when we slept in squalor—parties when things could have gone so horribly wrong.

If I'd spoken up Tom, Edie and Philippa would have had a better start in life. I let them down.'

'No!' The syllable was torn from him. 'You didn't let anyone down. You gave Tom and Edie and Philippa the right start in life, you kept them safe and you gave them love. I promise you, hand on heart, that you gave each one of them something incredibly precious. Something every baby and every child deserves. Your parents let you all down. The system let you down. *You* didn't let anyone down. This I know.'

'Thank you.' The words were polite, but she turned away as she spoke them to survey the vast expanse and he knew she had dismissed his words as so much bunkum.

'Why don't you ask them?'

That caught her attention and she twisted to face him, her breath white in the crisp cold air.

'I'm sure you would be able to trace them.'

'I won't do that.' Her chin tilted in a stubborn determination that spoke of a decision made.

'Why not? I understand the decision you made back then. But now... Now surely it would be good for you all to reconnect?'

She shook her head. 'I don't want to rock *their* boat. You should understand that. They are young adults now, and they have their own lives to lead. The last thing I want to do is complicate those lives. That's partly why I changed my name years ago—a clean break, a fresh start.'

'It sounds like there was a deep bond between you. I think they would want to hear from you.'

A sigh puffed from her lips and stricken eyes met his. 'They have each other and their adoptive parents. They don't need me.'

Ethan frowned, hearing the stubborn lilt to her voice. 'It's not about need, Ruby. Maybe they'd like to hear from you. Maybe they want to know what happened to you.'

He knew that if he could turn back time and somehow spend even five more minutes with Tanya he would move heaven and earth to do so.

His body tensed as Ruby turned again, rested her arms on the railing and stared out into the cold vastness of unforgiving beauty.

'It's a bit more complicated than that.'

'How?'

'What if I try and contact them and they say thanks, but no thanks? I've already lost them once and...' She gestured over the terrace rail. 'It was like plummeting into that chasm. I'm out of the pit now and I've got my life together. I can't face the prospect of falling back in.'

Her voice was small and lost and compassion touched him. 'It's okay to be scared. But that doesn't mean you shouldn't take the risk.'

'That's easy for you to say. You're never scared, and risk is your middle name. Given half a chance you'd leap off here and ski down the mountain.'

'That's different. That's about physical fear—it helps create a buzz; it's a good feeling. The fear of contact with your brother and sisters not working out is an emotional one, and it takes far more courage to overcome that then it does to climb a mountain.'

'But you don't have any emotional fears either.'

That was because he didn't let himself feel any emotion that he couldn't control. 'This isn't about me. This is about you. And I believe you should do this. Otherwise you're letting your fear conquer something that could make an enormous difference to your life and theirs.'

Her eyes shot anger at him—a dark blue laser. 'It's not your decision to make. All due respect, Ethan, but you don't know how this feels.'

'No, I don't. But...'

His turn now to look away, to absorb the vast

chill of white that would remain there long after he and Ruby had returned to normality.

'But what?'

The exasperation had left her tone and she shifted closer to him, placed a hand on his forearm. Her touch brought a soothing heat and somehow gave him the incentive to step into the chasm. To help Ruby make the decision he felt to be right.

'But I do know what it feels like to lose a sibling. I had a sister.' His voice cracked—the word was rusty with disuse. 'An older sister. Tanya. She died, and I would do pretty much anything to have the chance to see her again. So I am telling you, Ruby. Contact them. You have the chance of a future that has them in it. Take that chance.'

Her body stilled next to him and then she let out an exhalation of shock as her grip tightened on his arm. 'I am so sorry. I don't know what to say or do, but I am so very sorry.'

She closed the gap between them completely, so that her body pressed against his, and he took comfort from her closeness. For a long moment they stared out at the view, and then he heard her intake of breath.

'Do you want to talk about it?' she asked.

Did he? Disbelief rippled in his gut at the fact

he was even considering the hitherto impossible. But he was. Because he knew that once they left the Alps there would be no more of this. It was too emotional; too many layers were being unravelled and he couldn't risk his emotions escalating out of control.

But here and now the temptation to share his memories of Tanya nigh overwhelmed him, and images of his beautiful gentle sister streamed in his mind. He realised that he wanted Ruby to 'know' Tanya—to 'see' the sister he missed so much. Ruby had told him that talking about Tom, Edie and Philippa had reminded her of the good memories. Maybe Tanya deserved that—to be remembered.

His voice caught as he nodded his head. 'I think I do. But not here. Let's go back to the chalet.'

As they entered the chalet Ruby fought down the urge to throw herself onto his chest, wrap her arms around him and just hold him. Though… why not? For the next few hours at least she could be herself, could show feelings and emotions, and right now the desire to offer comfort overrode all else. But she knew that this was unmapped territory for both of them.

He shrugged his jacket off and hung it on a peg, watched her almost warily as she approached. Standing on tiptoe, she kissed his cheek, inhaled his woodsy scent, felt the solid bulk of his body against hers. She stepped back and took his hands in hers. The smile he gave was a little twisted, but his grasp tightened around hers as she tugged him towards the sofa.

'I'll light the fire,' he said.

Sensing that it would be easier for him to talk whilst in action, she nodded. 'That would be great. You want coffee?'

'No, thanks.'

He busied herself with the fire, loaded the logs, and Ruby curled up on the purple cushions, her whole being attuned to him.

'Tanya was three years older than me. Mum was always out—she worked so many jobs to make ends meet—and that made Tanya and I extra close. Tanya was...'

His deep tone faltered and he paused, scraped a match against the side of the box and lit the wood. Sat back on his haunches and gazed at the flicker of red and orange.

'She was so very gentle, so kind.' Wonder touched his voice. 'It was as if she was something rare and beautiful and fragile on that estate. She had chestnut hair, long and thick, and brown eyes, and the warmest smile in the world—the kind that made you feel like you could do anything.'

The fire whoomphed and caught, illuminated the planes of his features, touched with sadness now. Ruby slipped off the sofa, and as if aware of her movements he shifted, so that they both ended up on the floor with the sofa at their backs. Without speaking she placed a hand on his thigh, tucked her body next to his.

'She wanted to make something of her life. Her dream was to write, to travel, to see the wonders of the world. Mum encouraged her, and Tanya flourished—she loved books, absorbed information like a sponge. She'd tell me about all the countries out there and we'd hatch dreams of travel.'

'She sounds wonderful—and it sounds like you loved each other very much.'

No wonder Ethan had rejected love—he'd had the most important person in his world snatched by death. Yet the darkness of his expression told her that it was even worse than that.

'We did. It was Tanya who kept me on the straight and narrow for a long time. But as I got older it became harder for her.'

'What about your mum?'

'Mum was… Mum and I… It was difficult. I am the spitting image of my father. She hadn't actually wanted a second child with him and she never really engaged with me.'

Ruby felt her nails score her palm—it sounded as though Ethan felt he'd deserved the indifference she read from his words. 'That wasn't your fault.'

A shrug greeted this and she held her peace.

'No, but my behaviour was my own choice. The estate was my reality and I began to believe that Tanya's aspirations could never happen. I started to bunk off school, began to go off the rails. But Tanya held me in check; I would have done anything for her. If she'd let me.'

Foreboding touched Ruby, drizzled her skin with dread. 'What happened?'

'She was bullied. I didn't know—she didn't tell me, and we were at different schools by then. Tanya was doing A levels, and that meant a bunch of kids had it in for her. It started out as small-time stuff, teasing with a nasty edge, and then it became sabotage of homework, and then it became worse and worse. They stalked her, threatened her with rape, and eventually she couldn't take it any more. She killed herself.'

The words buzzed in the air like dark, malignant insects, and for a moment Ruby couldn't take in the enormity of his words. Once they hit her she raised her hand to her mouth to stifle the cry of protest. 'Ethan…' The anguish on his face was enough to make her weep.

'I found her. She'd overdosed—she'd found a stash of Mum's sleeping pills and swallowed the lot.' His voice jerked the words out, raspy and abuzz with a raw, jagged pain. 'At first I thought she was asleep, and then…'

Ruby swallowed the lump of horror that clogged her throat, pressed her lips together to stop herself from crying out. The image was so clear in her brain—she could only imagine how etched it was on his. A younger Ethan—lanky, tall, unsuspecting—calling his sister, entering the room… And then the awful paralysed second when he would have realised the grim truth and his life had changed for ever.

'Ethan…' Her voice was a whisper as compassion robbed her breath. 'I am so very sorry. I cannot imagine what you and your mother went through.'

The words were inadequate against such calamity, and she could only hope that the tragedy had brought mother and son closer.

'Mum was devastated. It was a dark time.'

For a long moment he stared into the flames and then he shifted slightly. Scored his palm down his face as if in an attempt to erase the memories.

'Do you think we could change topic? I'm kind of talked out.'

'Of course we can.'

Ruby tried to pull her thoughts together, her heart aching for what he had been through. For what he had told her and for the troubled relationship that he had with his mother. But now she wanted to lighten the mood, hoping that their conversation had been cathartic.

'How about a picnic and some board games?'

Surprise touched his face, and then his lips tipped into a small smile. 'That sounds perfect.' As she rose he followed suit and placed a hand on his arm. 'Thanks for listening.'

He cupped her jaw in his palms and dropped the lightest and sweetest of kisses on her lips. And her heart ached all the more.

As dawn slipped through the shutter's slats Ethan slipped quietly from the bed, pulled on his jeans and gazed down at Ruby, her cheek pillowed on her hand, her dark hair in sheer contrast to the white of the pillowcase and the cream of her skin. Her beauty touched him on a strata that he didn't want to identify and, turning away, he reached down for his shirt, thrust his arms into the sleeves and headed for the ladder.

Panic strummed inside him, made him edgy. Somehow Ruby had got right under his skin, and the idea caused angst to tighten his gut as he prowled the lounge and kitchen.

Memories of the past evening itched and prickled—they'd drunk cocoa in front of the lambent flames of the fire, talked of anything and nothing, laughed and philosophised. Then they'd gone to bed and... And there weren't words, truth be told, and he wasn't sure he even wanted to find any.

The panic grew—as if his actions had opened the floodgates. Letting her in had been a mistake, and nothing good could come of it. He wasn't capable of closeness.

'Ethan?'

He swivelled round, saw her at the top of the ladder. How long had she been there, watching him pace?

With an effort he forced his lips up into a relaxed smile. 'Morning!' he said, and his heart thumped against his ribcage as he took in her tousled hair, the penguin pyjamas.

Silence stretched into a net of awkwardness as she climbed down the ladder, paused at the bottom to survey him. Impulse urged him to walk over and carry her right back upstairs, and he slammed his hands into his jeans pockets and rocked back on his heels. No more impulses—because his emotions were already ricocheting off the Richter scale.

'Coffee?' he offered.

'Yes, please.'

Trying to keep his body rhythm natural, he headed to the kitchen. The endeavour was a fail and he passed her, breath held, unsure what to do, ultra-careful not to touch her. Yesterday he'd have teased her mercilessly about the penguins, dropped a kiss on her lips, taken her hand... Now he sidled past.

Ruby stood stock-still, one finger tugging a strand of hair. 'I'll...I'll go change,' she said, the words stilted, and relief rippled with regret touched his chest.

Because he knew she'd gone upstairs to armour herself in clothes. For this bubble of time she had been herself—no façade needed. Same for him. But now… Now it was time to go back to normal. Because being himself was too raw, too hard, too emotional. And emotion was not the way he wanted to go—he wanted the status quo of his un-rocked boat.

So he filled the kettle and assembled the ingredients for breakfast. The bread they had bought yesterday, the succulent strawberry jam, the pastries Ruby loved so much.

The sound of her shoes tapping on the wooden floor forced him to look up.

'Looks great,' she said, the words too bright, underscored with brittleness.

Her glorious hair was tamed into a sleek ponytail, not even a tendril loose. The knowledge sucker-punched him—never again would he run his fingers through those smooth silky curls, never again would he touch her soft skin, hear the small responsive gasp she made…

Enough.

A sudden urge to sweep the breakfast off the table, to get rid of the false image of intimacy, nearly overwhelmed him. The intimacy was over, and the sooner they exited this cloying atmosphere the better.

Too many emotions brewed inside him now, but at all costs he had to remember this was not Ruby's fault. If he had miscalculated it would not rebound on her. Instead he would haul back on all this feeling and return to professional normality. Though right now, in the line of her direct gaze, work seemed almost surreal. Which was nuts. Work was his life.

Jeez, Ethan.

Now he'd gone all drama king. Maybe he'd actually shed some brain cells these past days. In which case it was time to use the ones he had left. Fast.

No point in rueing the fact that he'd agreed to this fling in the first place. His eyes had been open to the fact that it would be different from his usual liaisons—he simply hadn't realised how that difference would play out. But there was no time for regrets. None at all. Regret was an indulgence—the important thing now was momentum.

With determination he lifted a croissant, went through the motions of spreading butter and jam. Then he glanced at his watch. 'We'll need to hit the road soon. I thought we could do a drive-round and get a visual of any areas or properties suitable for Caversham. I'll do a computer trawl whilst you pack up. Then maybe you can take over whilst I pack.'

'No problem.'

The cool near formality of her tone smote him even as he forced himself to pick up his coffee cup.

A gulp of coffee and she pushed her plate away. 'I'm on it.'

CHAPTER FOURTEEN

RUBY LOOKED AROUND the banqueting hall of Caversham Castle and tried to summon more than a token sense of pride and achievement. It looked fabulous, and she knew the sight would usually have prompted a victory dance or three around the room.

Actually it looked better than fabulous—she had worked flat-out the past two days, and all the work she had put in prior to Christmas had paid off. Medieval-style trestle tables fashioned from oak were arranged round the restaurant floor. The ceiling boasted an intricate mural depicting knights, princesses and acts of valour. The whole room seeped history, with maps of Cornwall through the ages and Cornish scenes from centuries ago adorning the walls.

Soon enough the room would be filled with the bustle of one hundred celebrity guests, the sound of troubadours and the scent of a genuine historic feast and Ruby knew the evening would be a success.

If only she cared.

She resisted the urge to put her head in her hands—of course she cared. This would be a career-tilting event—it would show the world that Ruby Hampton was the business. The restaurant at Caversham Castle would be launched in style, and she had little doubt that by the time they opened for normal custom in two weeks they would be booked up months in advance. Which was even better, because then she would be rushed off her feet.

Which would hopefully be the catalyst for the cessation of the stupid, mad feelings that swamped her every time she saw Ethan. The strange ache in her tummy when she wasn't with him...the stranger ache in her heart when she was. It would almost be preferable to discover that it was an ulcer rather than what she suspected—she missed him. Missed the Ethan she had glimpsed for forty-eight precious hours.

Unfortunately that Ethan had vanished—had donned the cloak of professionalism and left the building. How did he do that? Maybe the same way she did. After all, hadn't she been the epitome of a perfect restaurant manager? Could there be a possibility that he was hurting as she was?

But even if he was…what difference did it make? There could be no future. Her plan was to adopt and Ethan didn't want a family. Ethan didn't want *anything*.

In two days the ball would be over—it would be a new year and a new start. Ethan would waltz off to his usual business concerns and she would be able to get her head back together.

The back of her neck prickled and her whole body went to code red—a sure indicator that Ethan was in the vicinity.

'It's looking good,' he said. 'I need the final auction list, please. Rafael's on his way and he wants to look at it en route.'

'Sure. It's good of him to be auctioneer.'

'Yes.'

The terse edge of near indifference that veiled his tone made her foot itch with the urge to kick him even as she matched it. 'I'll email him the list straight away.'

'Ruby?'

The sound of Cora Brookes's even, well-modulated voice had her swivelling on her heel in relief. Cora, the new hotel administrator, had arrived two days before, and already Ruby was impressed by her smooth competence—though Cora had equally smoothly avoided all attempts at anything other than professional conversation.

'I thought you should see this.'

'What's up? Don't tell me the caterers have cancelled? Rafael Martinez has pulled out?'

For a second a faint look Ruby couldn't interpret crossed Cora's face. Then the redhead shook her head. 'Nothing like that. Why would he? It's great publicity for him… Plus it's not often a playboy like him gets to feature in a celebrity magazine in a charitable light.' She shook her head. 'Anyway, here you are.'

Ruby accepted the netbook and looked down at a celebrity magazine's website.

Breaking News!
Hugh Farlane engaged.
'This time it's the real thing,' Hollywood star proclaims.

What?
Disbelief churned in her tummy. She'd barely given Hugh a thought in the past days. Apart from

feeling a vague relief that he had obviously decided to stop offering her up as sacrificial goods to the press.

Mere weeks after his break-up with Ruby Hampton, now working within the Caversham Holiday Adventures empire, Hugh has announced his engagement to his long-term PA, Portia Brockman.

Portia? Beautiful, devoted to Hugh's interests, she'd worked for him for years—the woman had to know him better than anyone else, so why on earth would she marry him? Surely it was another stunt. Or... She looked down at the image of Portia, who was gazing up adoringly at Hugh. Maybe a better question would be did Portia *know* it was a stunt?

Next query—what was Ruby going to do about it?

Which led on to another question: if she thrust a spoke in Hugh's wheel what would he do? A flicker of fear ignited at the memory of his expression, taut with threat, as he'd ensured her silence.

It was a flicker she knew she had no choice but to ignore.

With a start she realised Ethan had removed the tablet from her grasp and was reading the article. A formidable frown slashed his brow as he handed it back to Cora.

'I'll have to go and sort this out,' Ruby said briskly. 'I'll get a train up to London—I should be back late this evening. Cora, thanks for bringing this to my attention. Can I leave a few things for you to do while I'm gone?'

'Of course.'

'Great. I'll catch you before I leave.'

Ruby nodded and turned, headed for the door.

'Hold on.' Ethan's stepped into her path, his tone peremptory.

'Yes?' Slamming to a halt, she tried to sound cool, as if her proximity to his chest, delectably covered in a white T-shirt, wasn't playing havoc with her respiratory system. Who wore T-shirts at the end of December, anyway?

'I'll come with you.'

'That is not necessary.'

Cora glanced from one to the other. 'Let me know what you need, Ruby. I'll be in my office or you can call me.'

Once the redhead had glided away, with admirable discretion, and the door had clicked shut, Ruby glared at Ethan.

'*So* not necessary,' she amended.

'I disagree—I told you I stand by my employees.'

All of a sudden a wave of pure white-hot anger flooded her—as if every molecule of built-up frustration from the past four days had all exploded into rage simultaneously.

'So you're going to hop on your charger and come and protect me because I am your *employee*?'

'What is wrong with that?'

'Everything. Everything is wrong with that.' Had he forgotten Christmas? Had some sort of brain transplant? 'Forget it. You have made it perfectly clear that you want our relationship to be professional.'

'We agreed that once we got back here we would revert to being professional.'

There was no arguing with that—if he took it a step further he might even point out that it had been *her* fool idea in the first place.

'You're right. So since my business with Hugh is *personal* I will deal with it myself.'

There was no indication that he'd even heard her. 'I don't want you to face him alone.'

'Why not? I'm sure I'll have to face plenty on my own when I adopt. There will be social workers and carers and teachers and who knows what else? Will you be there when it gets tough then?'

'That is hardly a valid argument.'

'It is extremely valid from my side.'

The air was tinged with exasperation as he folded his arms. 'That scenario is set in the future. This situation with Hugh is now. He's threatened you in the past, the man is a liar and a bully, and I don't see the problem with you accepting some support.'

Oh, crap!

As she stared at him, absorbed the frown that slashed his brow and the determined set of his mouth, drank in his sheer strength, the icy cold fingers of realisation dawned. Seeped into her soul. She knew exactly why this was a problem—she *wanted* Ethan to come with her. But she wanted his presence because he cared about her as person, not as an employee.

Panic squeezed her chest. She'd fallen for Ethan Caversham. Again. Or maybe she'd never got over him. This stubborn, generous, flawed man had called to something deep within her and her heart had responded without her permission.

She wanted him in her present *and* in her future.

Shock doused her veins, made her skin clammy. How had this happened? Ethan would never want a family. Would never change from being the workaholic, driven man he was. So why was her heart—the self-same heart that wasn't supposed to be involved—aching with a deep, bitter sting?

His frown deepened as he studied her expression and she desperately tried to think—tried to work out what to do with this awful, awesome knowledge.

Nothing. That was what she should do.

Ethan had made it more than clear that he had negative desire for a relationship, let alone a family. It wasn't his fault she'd been stupid enough to fall for him. If she told him how she felt he would recoil, and she wasn't sure she could bear that. Let alone the fact that it would make any work relationship impossible.

Maybe that would be impossible anyway. Maybe her best course of action would be to leave. Otherwise she would have to spend her life erecting a façade of lies, playing a part, watching him from afar, living in hope that one day he'd return her love. The idea made her tummy churn in revolt. It would be a replay of her childhood.

'Ruby?' There was concern in his voice now, as well as an assessing look in his blue-grey eyes that indicated the whirring of his formidable brain.

With an effort she recalled their conversation. 'Ethan, I need to do this by myself. Plus, tomorrow night is too important to blow—too important for kids like Tara and Max. You need to be here to supervise any last-minute glitches.'

He shook his head. 'Cora can cover that. So can Rafael.'

Somehow she had to dissuade him—all she wanted to do now was run. Achieve some space. Get her head together. Enough that she could hold the façade together for a while longer until she could find him a replacement restaurant manager.

'No. Cora and Rafael are great, but you need to be here. This is your show.' For a heartbeat she felt the sudden scratch of tears—this would be one of the last times they were together, and emotion bubbled inside her. 'You're doing such good here.'

Instinct carried her forward, so close to him that she could smell the oh-so-familiar, oh-so-dizzying woodsy scent of him. One hand reached out and lay on his forearm as she gazed up at him, allowed herself one last touch.

'Don't.' His voice low and guttural.

'Don't what? Tell the truth?'

He shook his head, stepped back so that her hand dropped to her side. 'Don't look at me like that. Don't make me a hero. Because I'm not.'

'I didn't say you were a hero. But you are a good man, and you do so much good. Why won't you acknowledge that and accept something good in your life.'

What was she doing? The sane course of action would be to get out of there at speed, but some small unfurling of hope kept her feet adhered to the floor.

'Whatever you did in the past can't change that.'

'You don't know about my past, Ruby.'

'Then tell me.'

For a long moment he looked deep into her eyes, and for a second she feared that he could read her thoughts, her emotions, could see the love that she was so desperately trying to veil.

His gaze didn't falter, though the clench of his

jaw and the taut stance of his body betrayed his tension.

'I told you that even before Tanya died I was beginning to go off the rails—I'd bunk off school every so often… I'd taken up smoking, graffitied the odd wall. But after she died I was so angry; I wanted vengeance on those bullies who'd made her last months on this earth a torment. But what could I do? I couldn't take them all on myself—they were a group, part of one of the most intimidating gangs on the estate. Mum was falling apart, and I was full of frustration and rage.'

Her lungs constricted as she imagined how the teenaged Ethan must have felt. So helpless, so alone. With a mother prostrate with grief and the sister he'd looked up to driven to take her own life.

'So it all went downhill. School became ancient history. I took up petty crime—shoplifting. I got into fights. I did dope…I drank. I swaggered around the estate like an idiot. I became everything Tanya would have abhorred.'

'Tanya would have understood. You were a child full of anger, pain and grief. Didn't your mum do anything?'

'She was too immersed in grief to notice.'

There was no rancour to be heard, but it seemed to Ruby that everything he had done must have been in an effort to make his mum notice—step in, *do* something. She couldn't bear the fact that he'd judged himself so harshly—that he couldn't see the plethora of mitigation around his actions.

'God knows what might have happened, but finally I got caught stealing from one of the high-street clothes stores. I went nuts—went up against the security officer. I lost it completely and they called in the cops. I was arrested, taken down to the police station, and they contacted my mother.'

'What happened?'

'As far as she was concerned it proved I'd morphed into my father. Reinforced her fear that history would repeat.'

'But…but she must have seen that this was different?'

His silence was ample testament to the fact that she hadn't, and the dark shadow in his eyes was further proof that neither had he. Foreboding rippled through her. 'What did she do?'

'Packed my stuff and handed me over to social services.'

Words failed her as anger and compassion inter-
twined—no wonder Ethan had judged himself as
guilty when his own mother had disowned him.

'Hey. Don't look like that. For Mum the loss of
Tanya was more than a tragedy—it was innately
wrong. It should have been me.'

'Did she say that?'

'Yes.'

The syllable was spoken as if it was to be expected and Ruby's heart tore.

'I get that. She had a point.'

'No, she did not!' The words were a shout, but
she couldn't help it.

'I let her down, Ruby. It is as simple as that. No
one made me act that way.'

'You were her *son*, Ethan—her child. You were
acting out of your own grief and anger.'

Ruby clenched her fists. Why was he being so
obdurate? But, of course, she knew the answer.
Hope. Why had she persisted in believing in her
own parents, long after they had proved they
would never change? Same answer. Hope.

'Have you seen your mum since?'

'No. She is still on the estate, and every year
I send her a cheque and a letter. Every year she

doesn't bank the cheque and she doesn't answer the letter.'

The unfairness, the tragedy of it, banded her chest. 'I understand that your mother had her own issues, but they were *her* issues. Would you ever do to a child what she did to you?'

Something flashed across his eyes and then he rubbed his hand down his face, made a derisive sound in his throat. 'Jeez. Let's end this conversation. Okay? I've come to terms with it all and it's no—'

'If you say it's no big deal I'll scream. It's a *huge* deal. You told me to fight for justice, that right and wrong matter. This matters, and this is injustice. Ethan, you told me you thought I would be a good parent.'

'You will be.'

'Well, a social worker told me once that damaged children like me repeat their parents' mistakes. I don't believe that has to be true and neither do you. That's why you want to help kids like Max and Tara—because you believe they deserve a chance. So do you.' Ruby hauled in breath. 'You have judged yourself and you've judged wrong. Whether your mum can see it or not, you're a good man, Ethan Caversham.'

For a second she thought she'd made some sort of impact, but then his broad shoulders lifted.

'Sure, Ruby. Whatever you want. I'm a good man.'

The self-mockery evident.

'You are. And you deserve love. Real, *proper* love.'

It all seemed so clear to her now—exactly why Ethan had his heart under such a guard, his emotions in lockdown. The only person who had loved him was the sister he felt he had let down—a sister he had lost so tragically. The mother who should have loved him had condemned him from birth.

'You do not have to be alone in that boat, Ethan. All family relationships do not have to end in tragedy. Love doesn't always have to go wrong.'

Discomfort etched his face, was clear in his stance as he rocked back on his heels, hands in his pockets. 'Leave it, Ruby.'

'I can't. You deserve love.' How could she make him see that? 'For what it's worth, I love you.'

His face was leached of colour; blue-grey eyes burned with a light she couldn't interpret. Eventually he stepped back.

'It's not love. It's what you felt for Hugh, for

Steve, for Gary. You said it yourself—you're not a good judge of character.'

'Ouch. That is below the belt.'

'No, it isn't. You don't love me—you want to heal me because you see me as broken. And I don't need to be healed. As for deserving love—that is irrelevant. I don't want love; I don't need love. I have come to terms with my past and I am moving forward. I'm not going to change. Any more than Gary, Steve or Hugh. So please don't waste your time thinking you love me. Find someone who will be good for you and to you. Someone who will father your children, whichever way you choose to have them. That man isn't me.'

The words were so final, so heavy, that she could feel her heart crack.

'Then I'd best get to London.'

What else was there to say?

CHAPTER FIFTEEN

THE CLICK OF the door unglued Ethan's feet from the floor, sent him striding forward, her name on his lips. Only to stop. What was he doing? He'd rejected her love so why was he following her? To do what?

His gut churned. He didn't want to hurt Ruby—hadn't wanted to a decade ago and didn't want to now. Somehow he had to make her see that he was right—she did not love him, whatever she believed. All he needed to do was convince her of that.

Maybe she'd work it out herself. See that every word he'd said was the truth. The past was over and he had come to terms with it. Had worked out that the best way forward was to move on, to channel his anger into becoming a success and using that success to help others. That worked for him—he didn't need love or a family. Didn't want love.

So why did he sound as if he was trying to convince himself?

The door swung open and Ethan swivelled round, his heart hammering in irrational hope that she had come back. Instead he saw Rafael Martinez, his expression creased in a small puzzled frown. 'A red-haired woman brought me here. Who is she?'

Pull it together, Ethan.

'Cora Brookes. My new hotel administrator.'

'I see.' Rafael frowned and rubbed his jaw. 'I had the distinct impression that Cora Brookes doesn't like me. She walked me here at the rate of knots and avoided all eye contact. Yet she looks familiar. Anyway it doesn't matter. I'm here, and ready to auction like a pro tomorrow. I also have a business proposition I want to discuss with you. But you look as though business is the last thing on your mind.'

He needed to get it together. This was Rafael Martinez and this was business.

'I'm fine. Happy to talk business. Why don't we go to my office?'

Get away from this banqueting hall with all its memories of Ruby.

Rafael's dark eyes surveyed him with what

looked like amusement. 'And how is the lovely Ruby Hampton?'

'Fine.' If Rafael was about to show even the most tepid interest in Ruby, Ethan had every intention of ramming his teeth down his throat. Business or no business. 'Why do you ask?'

'Whoa!' Rafael lifted his hands in the air. 'I was just curious. I get that she is off-limits.'

'Yes, she is.'

Rafael's eyebrows rose. 'Well, if you have an interest there you should know she has left the castle at speed—with a suitcase.'

Ethan paused as his brain attempted to compute the situation. Why would Ruby have taken a suitcase when she planned to return the same day? Unless she'd figured the journey there and back was too far? Needed some space? That must be it. Yet panic whispered in his gut.

There was a knock at the door and Cora entered, glanced at Rafael and then away again. 'Ethan. I'm not sure if I should mention this or not, but Ruby seemed upset and I'm not sure she's coming back.'

'What do you mean? It's the ball tomorrow.'

'I know.' Cora hesitated. 'It's just... She gave me the whole breakdown of the event in intricate detail—as if it was possible that she wouldn't be here. I mean…to be honest I can cover the admin side, because you and Ruby have planned it all down to the last detail. But I can't meet and greet or mingle with the guests. We agreed that.'

Her even voice held the hint of a quaver as her turquoise eyes met his and Ethan nodded. She was right. They had.

As if aware of Rafael's gaze as he studied her expression, Cora shifted so her back was to him. 'And, more importantly, as Ruby put all the work in I think she should be here to see the success I am sure it will be. I thought you should know.'

Ethan hauled in breath, tried to think.

Of course Ruby wouldn't leave.

You sure, Ethan?

The truth was the ball could go ahead without her and she knew it. It could be she was running—exactly as he had a decade ago. The irony was more than apparent.

Images of Ruby filtered through his brain. Her elfin features illuminated by enthusiasm, haunted by sadness, etched with compassion, lit up by desire. The gurgle of her laugh, the beauty of her smile… The idea of losing her, the idea that she might not return, sent a searing pain to his very soul.

Alongside that was fear...the terror of what it would feel like to let go, to allow his emotions full rein. Fear that he would somehow let Ruby down. If he allowed love to take hold he would screw it up, not be the man she deserved. That added up to a whole lot of scared.

The question now was what was he going to do about it?

Ruby approached the swish London hotel—the very same one where she had discovered Hugh's infidelity and perfidy in a double whammy. For a scant second she wondered why the idea of facing Hugh now didn't have the power to intimidate her. Possibly because she felt numb—had felt a cold, clammy sense of 'ugh' since she'd filled her suitcase and fled Caversham Castle.

Right now all she wanted was to get this over with, because she didn't want Portia to go through the same pain and disillusionment. In addition, it was about time she stood up to Hugh Farlane.

As she entered the imposing lobby—all fancy uniformed staff, marble and fluted pillars—one of Hugh's assistants rushed over to her.

'Come with me,' he said, his eyes roving the area. 'We don't want any bad publicity.'

'Hi, Greg. Good to see you again. Thanks for arranging this.'

The young man flushed. 'Sorry. It's good to see you too. But Hugh is very emphatic that I get you up there fast.'

'So he hasn't decided how to spin it yet?'

Greg declined to answer, shifting from foot to foot in an agony of discomfort, and then hustled her to the lift.

Once inside the sleek metal box, she felt a sliver of worry permeate the anaesthetic of hurt. Hugh Farlane had the power to crush her like an insignificant bug, and she didn't have Ethan's protection to fall back on now. In her own mind at least she was no longer a Caversham employee.

The irony was that she'd come full circle.

No! Not true. Weeks before she hadn't had the courage to stand up to Hugh. Now she did. In the past weeks she'd learned so much—on a professional *and* a personal level.

Before, the thought of any contact with her siblings had been an impossibility—now the idea seemed feasible. Because Ethan had shown her a new perspective. Somehow he had shown her her own inner strength. Which was a further irony. Because now she would have need of that strength to get over Ethan.

Not now. Put the pain aside and channel that inner power.

Her vertebrae clicked as she straightened up. The lift doors swooshed open and she stepped forward and followed Greg along the plushly carpeted floor to the ornate door of the penthouse suite.

'Good luck,' Greg murmured as he knocked and then faded discreetly away.

The click as the door swung open set her heart pounding but she managed a smile.

'Ruby…' Hugh stepped forward, the familiar smile full of charm on his lips. 'Great to see you. Come right on in.'

Could the man have had some sort of amnesia attack?

'Drop the charm, Hugh,' she said. 'I've come here to give you fair warning.'

'Of what?'

'If this is another scam I won't stand by and let it happen. I will not let you do it to Portia.'

A roll of his deep brown eyes. 'And what exactly do you think you can do to stop me? Wait.' He raised his hand. 'I can answer that for you. There is nothing you can do. Portia believes in me, and as far as she is concerned you are a gold-digging vixen. And that's the way it's going to stay. In fact…' A casual shrug accompanied his words. 'It may get a bit heated for you in the press again. We'll be giving interviews, and Portia does feel very strongly about you.'

'That's a joke, right?' Her imagination went into boggled mode. 'You want me to take the flak *again*?'

'Yes.' Hugh smiled—a smile that would reduce half the population to its knees but left her utterly unmoved. 'That's not a problem, is it?'

'What if I say it is?'

Goodbye to the smile and any pretence of charm. 'Then you'll leave me no choice. I'll take you for everything you have. You'll lose your job like a shot. You may think Ethan Caversham will protect you, but how long do you think he will do that if I really go to war? Threaten to get one of my friends to sue him?'

'Sue him for what?' Disbelief and a smidge of fear touched her.

'For improper safety procedures—I could rig an accident, no sweat.' Tipping his hands in the air, he switched the smile back on. 'I don't *want* to do it, Rube. I don't… But I need this marriage to happen. Those Forsythe sisters have got a bit suspicious…my agent is on my back again. Yada-yada.'

'In other words you've reverted to type,' Ruby interjected.

'Whatever. Point is, Portia is my salvation.'

Ruby stared at him, and suddenly so much seemed clear to her. 'Ethan will never cower before your so-called might. And neither will I. Not any more. So I suggest you tell Portia the truth. Because if you don't, I will. And if you lie about me one more time in the papers then I will call you on it. I will give an interview of my own and then if you want to retaliate you go for it. Bring it on.'

A burst of adrenalin shot through her system. Ethan was right—the only way to deal with a bully was to stand up to him.

Hugh's eyes narrowed. 'I could drag you through the mud.'

'Go right ahead. But I will not let you do this to Portia. Or to me. I want you to tell her the truth and I want you to issue a statement saying that we have sorted our differences and you were mistaken about my gold-digging tendencies.'

He deflated before her eyes, sank onto a chair. 'You don't understand. I'm scared I'll lose my career...'

'Then fight for it. Clean up your act. Change. But do it for real and fight clean.'

Even as she spoke the words it occurred to her that she had hardly put her own money where her lips were. With Ethan she'd accepted rejection as if it were only to be expected. She hadn't put up so much as a vestige of fight—had let him write off her love as false.

Was that the person she'd become? Sure, years ago she'd lost the fight to keep her family together, but that did not mean she had to lose every fight. The truth was, it was easier, less painful, to expect and accept defeat. After all, the harder you fought the more you risked losing.

A hard rock of determination formed inside her. 'Your choice, Hugh. I've got to go.'

'Okay. I'll do it.'

Ruby nodded, already en route to the door. Her thoughts swirled as she figured out how long it would take her to get back to Cornwall. Should she call first? Text? Email?

The elevator felt claustrophobic, stupidly slow, and she jogged from foot to foot as impatience seized her.

Finally the doors opened and she stepped outside—and there was Ethan.

Thank goodness. Ethan's heart thumped against his ribcage as Ruby erupted from the elevator—he'd already paced a layer off the marble floor of the lobby.

Ruby skidded to a stop and stared at him as if he could be some sort of hologram. 'Ethan?'

'In the flesh.'

'But…what are you doing here?'

'We need to talk. How did it go with Hugh?'

'Good. All sorted. He'll tell Portia the truth and issue an apology to me.'

'That's fabulous, Ruby.'

'Is that why you came here? To check I could cope with Hugh?' Wariness tinged her expression now as she tugged at an errant strand of hair.

'Nope. Were you planning on coming back to Caversham Castle?'

'No. But…'

Ethan held a hand up, not sure he could bear to hear any more. Fear strummed him. She had believed the sheer baloney he had spouted earlier. Somehow he had to convince her to give him another chance.

'Not here. We need to talk properly.'

She nodded. 'There are loads of cafés round here. Or...'

'It's okay. I have it covered. Come on.'

Within seconds of leaving the lobby Rafael's loaned car glided to a halt in front of them. The chauffeur climbed out and opened the car door for Ruby, who slid inside with a puzzled look.

'Why didn't you drive your own car?' she asked.

'Actually, Rafael lent me his helicopter, as well as Robert and this car, to meet me on arrival.'

'You *flew* here from Cornwall?' Her eyes widened and a half-laugh dropped from her lips. 'Why?'

Ethan shrugged. 'Impulse. I needed to see you. To apologise and...'

Her eyes narrowed. 'Apologise for what?'

Here goes.

Time to put himself on the line. Along with some emotional honesty. 'For my reactions. I panicked. Just like I did ten years ago. I've been alone a long time; the only person who has ever got close has been you. Ten years ago I ran. I told myself I did it for you, because I could see that you had developed a misguided crush on me, but in reality I panicked.'

'And this time?' The question was soft, almost tentative.

Clenching his hands round his knees, he hauled in breath. 'This time I don't want to run, and I don't want you to run. For ten years I have avoided emotion, locked it down because I associated emotion with bad choices, rejection and tragedy. I decided to channel my anger and use it to create momentum—to build Caversham into something bigger and bigger, to allow me to do good via charitable efforts.'

'And you succeeded—you turned your life around.'

A twist of her body and she faced him now, her face illuminated in the dusky light of the limo's interior, her cinnamon scent whirling in his head.

'You should be proud of that.'

'I am. But the whole time I have been scared of emotion, scared of rocking the boat, because I thought my whole new life would tumble down. These past few weeks you have shown me that doesn't have to happen. With you I have run the gamut of emotions—each day I have felt more and more. Caring, desire, happiness, sympathy, a need to give and take comfort. You've unlocked something inside me. You've helped me remember Tanya as she deserves to be remembered—not just with bitterness and guilt, but with the memory of all the good she did in my life. You've let me look down the dark tunnels of the past and realise that along with the darkness there was also light. And there's something else you did too...'

'What?'

Her voice caught and fear and anticipation rollicked through him.

'You taught me how to love. I love you, Ruby.'

For a heartbeat her expression registered no more than shock, and the fear escalated. What if she had changed her mind—realised that loving him was foolhardy? Then he would change her mind if it took him his whole life to do it. Then her expression morphed into a smile that touched and warmed him as she launched herself across the limo seat and into his arms.

'I love you too. So very, *very* much. And I swear to you it is nothing to do with a need to heal you. Because I don't need to do that—I love you exactly as you are. You're kind and generous and caring and stubborn and demanding and deep and complicated, and I love you for all those traits. You don't need to change for me.'

She nestled onto his lap, her hands cupping his jaw, and he felt a thrill of happiness. This woman loved him, and he knew he was the luckiest man in the universe.

'That realisation has been an epiphany for me. You see, all my life I have associated love with need. I wanted to be needed. My parents didn't love me enough to change their lifestyles for me, so I equated someone loving me with them being willing to change for me. Because that would give me self-worth. You've taught me how to have self-worth all by myself. You've shown me how to be brave, to stand up for what is right, and you've taught me to risk again—to risk rejection, to risk pain, because sometimes that is the right thing to do. So you don't have to change to prove your love or mine. I love *you*.'

'And I love you.'

He could quite cheerfully have continued in this conversational vein all day. His heart gave a happy jump and his whole body fizzed with a joy he could barely believe.

The limo glided to a stop and he dropped a kiss on her lips. 'Now that is sorted you need to come with me.'

'Where to?'

'Wait and see.'

The door opened and Ruby scrambled off Ethan's lap, sneaking a quick glance at the impassive face of the chauffeur and figuring he'd probably seen worse as Rafael Martinez's driver.

She looked around in an attempt to work out where they were. Not that it mattered—all that mattered was Ethan's proximity and the sheer sense of wonder that doused her. Ethan *loved* her. The urge to cartwheel, to grab passers-by and tell them of her sheer happy feelings nigh overwhelmed her.

Instead she looked round and took in a tree-lined canal, with moored narrowboats of all colours bobbing up and down on the water. Cream Georgian architecture abounded, and the whole area felt like a quirky peaceful oasis in the midst of London's sprawl.

A quick tour of her mental knowledge told her they were in Little Venice.

'Come on,' Ethan said.

His grin was so boyish, so relaxed, that her heart threatened to burst.

'Close your eyes.'

Ruby scrunched her eyes shut and wrapped her fingers round Ethan's capable hand, anticipation unfurling as he guided her along the pathway.

'Okay. You can look.'

A small gasp escaped her lips as she surveyed the boat—gaudy, cheerful, bright red. It looked as though it had a personality all its own.

'Ta-dah!' Ethan beamed at her. 'Welcome to the *Oasis*. Fifty-eight feet long, six foot ten inches wide, she'll be able to take us all over England's canals.'

The grin dropped from his face, to be replaced by a serious expression, his blue-grey eyes full of passion and determination. 'It's symbolic. I want you on board my boat, Ruby, and I don't care how much it rocks or rolls or even if it capsizes, as long as we are on it together.'

The words caused a prickle of tears and he looked at her, consternation written all over his face.

'Hey, don't cry!'

'I can't help it. That is so beautiful and…' She gulped. 'I can't believe you bought a boat!'

'Come and see.'

Ruby followed him inside and felt an instant sense of home. The interior had a clean, homey, compact feel, with the space used to incredible effect. The kitchen area gleamed with pine, and as she explored she gave a small gurgle of delight at the dexterity of the storage space. Already she could picture rustling up meals as they chugged along England's canalways.

Walking further in, she saw the tiny but functional bathroom and shower room. 'There's even a dining area!'

'Well, meals are an important consideration. And look—when we don't need the table it can be folded away and we convert it into a lounge. Plus there are two cabins—a double room and a twin. Tight fit, but...'

Ruby stilled. 'Why the twin bedroom?' she asked.

'Because one day I hope that we will have children. Adopted or birth or a mixture of both.'

His words caused her to freeze, unsure whether to believe him or not, and needing him to understand that she truly loved him for himself. Only him. That he was way more than enough.

'You don't have to say that. I meant what I said.

You are who I want. I want my future to be with you—to wake up every day wrapped in your arms.'

'I get that, Ruby, but you have changed me. You've opened my heart. And I have enough love in there for you and for children. Of course I'm scared—scared I'll mess it up, terrified I'll let them down—but I also know I will strive every day to be the best parent I can. Because you were right earlier. I don't blame my mum for what she did, but I could never do that to my child. I would never give up and I would never stop loving them. I'll be there for them, Ruby. I swear I will.'

'There is no doubt in my mind, or in my heart.'

Of course he was scared—after his childhood how could he not be? But she knew that Ethan would be a wonderful dad, and she wanted to whoop with joy that he too wanted a family.

'I know you will be a wonderful dad, and I so want us to be a family. I've decided to try to trace Tom, Edie and Philippa as well. Make some new memories.'

The idea still scary, but with Ethan by her side, there to catch her if she fell, as she would be there for him, it seemed less daunting.

'I'll support you one hundred per cent. In this and everything, Ruby. Now and for ever.'

His smile was so full of love her breath hitched in her throat.

He gestured towards a corner of the lounge area. 'And right now why don't you have a look in your stocking?'

'Huh?' Following the trail of his hand, her eyes alighted on a small Christmas tree, still in its pot, decorated with silver strands of tinsel and red, purple and gold decorations. Pinned next to it was a bulging striped stocking, with a candy cane poking out of the top.

'I know it's not Christmas anymore. But I figured there was still some Christmas magic left in the air,' he said.

There were those tears of joy. *Again*. 'How on earth did you manage to do all this?'

A grin and the wicked wiggle of his eyebrows banished her tears in favour of a chuckle.

'Consider me all-powerful. Actually, it wasn't too hard. The helicopter only took an hour or so… Rafael's driver picked me up at Battersea… A few stops on the way and then straight here to Little Venice, where the ex-owner of *Oasis* waited. I cleaned the place, set up the tree, and then I went back to the hotel to wait for you.' Eagerness lit his expression as he shifted from foot to foot. 'Come on—open it.'

Unhooking the stocking, Ruby sank onto the cushioned sofa and dived her hand inside. Pulled out a heart-shaped box of chocolates, a gorgeous bath bomb that exuded lavender and chamomile, a pair of fluffy woolly socks... And then, nestled in the toe, her questing fingers found a box.

Heart pounding, mouth parched, she tugged it out and opened it. Inside was a ring—a glorious cluster of sapphires and diamonds.

'Sapphires to match the sparkle of your eyes,' Ethan said. 'Diamonds because diamonds are for ever. Will you marry me, Ruby?'

'Yes.' The assent dropped from her lips and happiness blanketed her as he slid the ring onto her finger. 'It's *so* beautiful.'

'Not as beautiful as you. Now, look up.'

There above them was a sprig of mistletoe, and as Ethan's lips covered hers she knew that her happiness was complete. They would sail their boat together over the horizon, into a life that would hold ups and downs, rain and sunshine.

But she knew with all her heart that their love would ride every swell, weather every storm and bask in each ray of happiness.

EPILOGUE

The Caversham Castle Ball

RUBY FELT AS if she were walking, floating, *dancing* on air as she greeted each and every guest at the ball. Time seemed spun with the shining threads of pure happiness as she rested her gaze on Ethan, listened to his speech—his words powerful, emotive and drenched with compassionate belief in his cause.

'He's a good man.'

Ruby turned to see Cora Brookes by her side.

'He is.'

Instinctively she looked down at her left hand, even though she and Ethan had decided to keep their engagement under wraps until the end of the ball. Ruby had insisted that the ball was about fundraising—she didn't want to dilute the impact in any way.

They watched as Ethan introduced Rafael and the tall, dark-haired man took the podium; his aristocratic lips upturned in a captivating smile—within minutes he had them riveted by his words as the bids climbed to outrageous heights.

Cora gazed at him. 'He has the charm of the devil,' she murmured under her breath.

'He's putting it to a good cause.'

'Men like Rafael Martinez only have one cause—their own.' A strand of bitterness tinged Cora's tone. 'I'm surprised he and Ethan are so close.'

Ruby frowned. 'Ethan sees the good in everyone, and he is a great believer in second chances. Plus, you shouldn't believe everything you read in the papers. Trust me on that. Unless, of course, you know Rafael?'

Cora hesitated. 'No,' she said finally. 'I don't.' A perfunctory smile and then she gestured towards the door. 'I'll go and check the champagne is ready for midnight.'

Ruby turned as Ethan headed towards her.

'All okay, sweetheart?' he asked. 'Why the frown?'

'I was just wondering why Cora doesn't like Rafael...'

'Lots of people don't like Rafael. But he has his good points. Or at least I hope he does. He and I have decided to invest in a business venture together. Spanish vineyard holidays.'

'Maybe we could honeymoon in Spain?'

Ethan shook his head, his expression serious. 'We are *not* going on a working honeymoon, my love. I have way better plans than that, I promise you.'

'I can hardly wait.'

He grinned down at her—a smile that lit his face—and his blue-grey eyes were flecked with a love that stole her breath.

'I think Rafael has everyone's attention,' he murmured. 'So let me snag us a glass of champagne…I want to toast our future under the stars.'

And as he twined his strong hand in hers Ruby basked in the healing lessons learnt from the past, the wondrous glow of joy of the present, and the glorious promise of the future.

* * * * *

MILLS & BOON®
Large Print – April 2016

The Price of His Redemption
Carol Marinelli

Back in the Brazilian's Bed
Susan Stephens

The Innocent's Sinful Craving
Sara Craven

Brunetti's Secret Son
Maya Blake

Talos Claims His Virgin
Michelle Smart

Destined for the Desert King
Kate Walker

Ravensdale's Defiant Captive
Melanie Milburne

The Best Man & The Wedding Planner
Teresa Carpenter

Proposal at the Winter Ball
Jessica Gilmore

Bodyguard...to Bridegroom?
Nikki Logan

Christmas Kisses with Her Boss
Nina Milne

MILLS & BOON®
Large Print – May 2016

The Queen's New Year Secret
Maisey Yates

Wearing the De Angelis Ring
Cathy Williams

The Cost of the Forbidden
Carol Marinelli

Mistress of His Revenge
Chantelle Shaw

Theseus Discovers His Heir
Michelle Smart

The Marriage He Must Keep
Dani Collins

Awakening the Ravensdale Heiress
Melanie Milburne

His Princess of Convenience
Rebecca Winters

Holiday with the Millionaire
Scarlet Wilson

The Husband She'd Never Met
Barbara Hannay

Unlocking Her Boss's Heart
Christy McKellen

0416 Rom LP